Welcome to the darker side of romance

12 SHADES OF
SURRENDER

Two volumes of intense, unforgettable
short stories from top erotic authors, including
Megan Hart, Tiffany Reisz, Saskia Walker
and Portia da Costa

12 SHADES OF SURRENDER

UNDONE

MEGAN HART
ANNE CALHOUN
ALISON TYLER
EMELIA ELMWOOD
EDEN BRADLEY
SASKIA WALKER

Mills & Boon, an imprint of Harlequin (UK) Limited,
Eton House, 18-24 Paradise Road, Richmond, Surrey TW9 1SR

12 SHADES OF SURRENDER: UNDONE
© Harlequin Enterprises II B.V./S.à.r.l. 2012

The Challenge © Megan Hart 2010
Under His Hand © Anne Calhoun 2011
Cuffing Kate © Alison Tyler 2012
The Envelope Incident © Emelia Elmwood 2009
Night Moves © Eden Bradley 2010
Going Down © Saskia Walker 2012

ISBN: 978 0 263 90462 8

084-0812

Printed and bound by
CPI Group (UK) Ltd, Croydon, CR0 4YY

CONTENTS

The Challenge

By Megan Hart

Megan Hart is the award-winning and multi-published author of more than thirty novels, novellas and short stories. Her work has been published in almost every genre, including contemporary women's fiction, historical romance, romantic suspense and erotica. Megan lives in the deep, dark woods of Pennsylvania with her husband and children, and is currently working on her next novel. You can contact Megan through her website at www.MeganHart.com.

"You're late. Again." Katie Donato barely glanced away from her laptop as Dean Manion slipped the nonfat, sugar-free white chocolate latte onto her desk and his lean, long body into the chair next to hers.

"But I brought lattes."

She glanced at him then, taking in the smug grin, the artfully careless hair, the slightly loosened tie. "You know, traffic is a good excuse for being late. Lost car keys. Forgetting you had to pick up your favorite suit from the dry cleaner's, even. But not last-minute blow jobs from the dude at the Copy Cabana."

Dean laughed and sipped from his own cup. "Not last-minute, not Copy Cabana."

At this, she swiveled in her chair to study him. "Don't tell me you had a sleepover last night?"

Dean grinned in answer and drank deeply. "Ahhh, sweet caffeine. I'm going to need it."

"Is that your subtle way of saying you were up all night fucking?" Katie lifted a brow and sipped at the drink, then tipped the cup toward him. "This is a peace offering but it still doesn't let you off the hook. We have a meeting with Smith and Simon in half an hour and I've been here since eight putting this proposal together."

"Sorry." Dean's brows knitted and he leaned forward to rub his knees against hers, but Katie pushed him away with a laugh.

"Stop. I'm not some eighteen-year-old, just-out-of-the-closet emo-banged pretty boy. I'm immune to your wiles."

"Bullshit." Dean said this with the utter and absolute confidence of a man who oozes sensual appeal and knows it. He leaned back and propped his feet, shod in expensive Italian leather, on her desk.

Katie shoved them off. "It's not bullshit. I know you too well, Dean. You're like a Lladró figurine. Pretty to look at but too expensive to be practical and not at all useful."

"Hey." He frowned at this and set his cup on the desk to lean toward her again. He touched her knee. "The fuck's that supposed to mean?"

Katie, spreadsheet completed, hit the Print button and stood to smooth the wrinkles in her skirt.

"It means you should've been here at eight this morning to do your part of this project and you weren't, because you were too busy getting your dick sucked."

She wasn't angry–not really. Annoyed but not furious. She'd worked with Dean long enough to understand him, so when he sidled in late to work with a latte for her, she knew better than to be surprised. Didn't mean he was free of blame, though.

"I said I'm sorry."

She knew he meant it, even as she knew without even looking at him he was giving her a patented Dean sexy stare guaranteed to bring most anyone to their figurative knees. She pulled the papers from her printer and stapled them, then slipped them into the presentation folder she'd carefully prepared. She gathered the rest of her materials while he watched in silence, but damn it, lost it all when she could no longer stifle the yawn that had been doing its best to sneak out of her.

"Ha!" Dean stood, looming. "What's that?"

Katie feigned innocence and swigged coffee. "What?"

"You yawned." Dean had no problems invading anyone's personal space if it benefited him, but he was one of the few who could get away with such a thing with Katie. Now he sidled up close, blocking her retreat by pressing a thigh against hers to keep her pinned with the desk at her back. "Up late?"

Katie bit hard on the inside of her cheek to keep from giving in to a grin. "None of your business."

"Katie," Dean said in a low, sultry tone. "Of course it's my business. Who was he? Guy from the dry cleaner's? The gym? Don't tell me he's that loser from college who looked you up on Connex."

"Time for the meeting."

It was useless, and Katie should've known better. Dean put out one long arm and kept her from moving past him. "Spill it."

She sighed. "Fine. You don't know him because I've never mentioned him before. I met him in a coffee shop a few months ago."

"The Green Bean? Which guy?"

"No. The Morningstar Mocha. And you wouldn't know him, he's straight." At least she thought Jimmy was straight. She hoped he was.

"A few months ago? You've been holding out on me?" Dean frowned. "Damn."

"Not holding out." Katie rested her butt on the

desk, an eye on the clock, and drank her coffee. "There isn't anything to tell you. Unlike you, I don't bang just any guy who comes along."

Dean put a hand over his heart. "That hurts. You act like I don't have standards."

It was nice to have a friend good enough to understand that a single raised brow meant so much. "Uh-huh."

He leaned against the filing cabinet across from her. "He kept you up late. That's something."

"We weren't fucking, Dean."

He made a face. "Why the hell not?"

"I don't know," Katie teased. "Maybe I'm wrong and he is gay."

Dean snorted into his coffee and tilted his head to study her. "You like him?"

"You like the guy you were with this morning?" She deflected the question easily enough.

"I like all the guys I'm with, at least at the time."

Katie ticked off the list on her fingers. "You let him sleep over and were late to work because of him. Granted, that doesn't mean much, but add to that the fact you haven't been describing every inch of his cock to me in precious, explicit detail, and I'm pretty sure that means you like him."

Dean's gaze shifted. Ah, she was spot-on. Wow.

"Dunno what you mean."

"You only keep quiet about the dudes you like, which are few and far between lately." Actually, there hadn't been any. Katie kept the tone light, not wanting to bring up old flames just for the sake of needling her friend–there was plenty to tease Dean about without bringing Ethan into it.

"Sure, I like him. I like lots of stuff."

Katie laughed. "I know you do."

With this laid out between them, Dean seemed satisfied. "So long as he's not that douche from Connex. That guy was bad news."

Katie laughed at the way Dean bristled on her behalf. "Umm…no. I wouldn't even fuck him with your dick. C'mon, move that pretty ass. Time to shine."

"We have a few minutes."

Katie sighed again. An old argument. She liked to be prompt, even early. Dean preferred to make a grand entrance. She eyed his practiced pout. "I told you, that doesn't work on me."

"It works on everyone."

This was very close to true. "Only because everyone else doesn't know you like I do. All promise, no delivery."

Dean leered, once more leaning so close Katie could get a full whiff of his delicious cologne. "Shut your mouth! The fuck you mean, no delivery? I deliver."

Katie leaned, too, so her breath would tickle his earlobe. "No, babe. That ass and that smile promise a lot but Dean Manion only delivers to addresses on Penis Avenue. Vagina Street's out of your delivery zone, remember?"

He turned his face half an inch so his lips brushed her neck. "Just because I don't doesn't mean I couldn't."

At this boast, so typical, Katie burst into laughter loud enough to make her happy she had her own office with a closed door. She pushed at his chest. "Please. You've never fucked a woman. Have you ever even *kissed* a woman?"

"I've kissed you," he reminded her, letting her push him away but not making it easy.

"A New Year's Eve kiss under mistletoe. Besides," Katie said as she gave his tie a fond yank, "there was no tongue. Doesn't count."

"Doesn't mean I couldn't," Dean repeated stubbornly.

Katie cast another glance at the clock. Fifteen minutes to make it from her office, down the hall, up three floors in the notoriously slow elevator, down another two corridors to get to the meeting room. "Look, your reputation as a sex bomb is safe with me. I swear I will never reveal to all the women crushing on you that you'd rather get a paper cut on your tongue than eat pussy."

She laughed again at his outraged expression. "Don't act like it's not true. I've seen you with the girls in reception, the ones who always give you doughnuts. You can whore yourself for a bear claw all you want, but when it comes right down to it, you won't put out."

Dean was the part of their team who came up with the brilliant ideas; Katie figured out how to put them into action. Dean orchestrated the flash and bang while Katie made sure all the pieces fit into place. Yet it was Dean who fought the hardest to win the accounts, even when Katie's careful financial summaries determined the risk wasn't worth the effort. Dean who worked long hours ripping apart campaigns and sewing them back together until nobody could possibly offer something better. The same competitive edge that made him killer at racquetball drove him in his work, too, just as Katie's intrinsically neat and tidy personality did in hers.

She'd just tapped Dean's warrior nature. She saw it in his eyes and stance, so briefly fierce she'd have stepped back from it if the desk hadn't already been under her butt. Any other man in the office–hell, anywhere–who gripped her hips and pulled her close up on his crotch that way, who ran his mouth along the curve of her neck to find her ear and breathe heat into it —any other man would've earned a knee to the nuts and possibly the heel of her hand into his Adam's apple.

Instead, Katie tensed under Dean's practiced touch, head tipping to give him greater access. There was no denying he was scrumptious. Probably more so because they were such good friends, and she knew his quirks. Most definitely because he was gay and triggered the "never gonna get it" hormone. Now she closed her eyes while he ran his lips lightly over her skin.

"This is so out of the boundaries of appropriate workplace behavior it's not even funny," she murmured.

He moved away, not quite enough. "Since when have I ever been appropriate?"

"This is true," Katie said, amused to hear the sex-syrup tone of her own voice. God, it had been too long since a man had put his hands on her. "However, it doesn't mean you could make me come."

Disgruntled, Dean stepped back. "You think it would be so easy to get me off?"

"I do, actually. Now c'mon, shake that oh-so-fine ass, please. We really have to move."

Dean crossed his arms, still looming over her. "What makes you think that?"

"Because I'm looking at the clock."

"No." Dean shook his head. "That I'd be so easy to get off, but you wouldn't. What makes you so sure?"

He was, Katie saw with genuine surprise, seriously wounded. She tugged his tie gently. "Because you have a penis, sweetie, and penises are notoriously easy to please. And I like sucking cock. I'm sure if you closed your eyes, you'd never know my mouth was attached to a set of breasts and a cunt. On the other hand, the fact you've never made love to a woman and aren't turned on by women, would probably mean that providing me with the same favors wouldn't be as successful."

She paused, deciding to go for the truth simply because Dean was a friend and a good one, at that. "And because I have a hard time getting off with straight men who are into me. I think managing an orgasm with a guy I knew was cringing the whole time would really be impossible."

"Is that a challenge?"

"Oh, for Pete's sake. No."

Dean gave her the full force of his flirting grin, the one she'd seen slay the girl who brought around the bagels, random guys on the street and everyone in between. "You're afraid to take me up on it?"

"Are you suggesting I...fuck you?" Katie didn't even look at the clock this time. The idea was intriguing. Tempting, even. It wasn't like she'd never wondered what it was like to get in Dean's pants. And to be the first woman to ever have him?

Fucking delicious.

"I'm saying we should fuck each other. We'll see who gets who off first." Dean ran a hand through his hair, pushing it away from his eyes. "And fastest."

"Sex is always such a game to you."

"And that's wrong...because...?"

"Because we're late, for one thing," she said sternly. "For real, this time. Let's go. If you want this account–"

"Say yes, Katie."

She looked him up and down, taking in every detail. She knew every inch of Dean already, having spent so many hours with him, and suspected he was probably as familiar with her. She looked at him with new eyes, now. She'd gone to bed with men she was less attracted to than she was to Dean, so really, where was the issue? Sex was with him was unlikely to lead to one of those three-in-the-morning talks about what it all meant, and if it did, both of them would be fools. At the very worst, she'd be proven right, and even with that, how could getting a full serving of the delicious, deep-dish pie of gorgeous that was Dean be wrong?

"You're on," Katie said.

"You did what?" Jacob, standing at the sink and rinsing a pot of steaming hot pasta, turned so fast a few strands of limpid spaghetti slopped over the sides.

Dean leaned against the counter, bottle of beer he hadn't yet tasted in one hand. "You heard me."

"Oh, I heard you." Jacob turned back to the sink and ran cool water over the pasta before dumping it all into the bowl. "I just can't believe it. You're going to have sex with a woman?"

Now Dean drank. "Yeah."

He watched Jacob's shrug, wondering whether that meant the other man was dismissing the possibility or expressing jealousy. Or maybe Jacob didn't give a shit, Dean thought, tasting the richness of the beer. Would he have cared if Jacob had told him the same thing? What would Dean have said?

Jacob turned again and brought both Dean's bottle and Dean's hand to his mouth to drink. He licked his lips, then mirrored Dean's stance against the counter, both hands gripping the marble at his sides. "And she agreed to it?"

"Of course she did." Dean drank again and set the bottle on the counter to grab Jacob's wrist and pull him closer. Jacob stood just an inch shorter, his sandy hair cropped in a buzz cut shorter than Dean usually liked. Eyes bluer, ass just a little too flat. But a mouth made of perfect, one Dean had no trouble kissing or fucking.

Jacob opened his mouth when Dean kissed him. Their tongues teased languidly until Dean slid a hand down to cup Jacob's crotch. Then Jacob drew in a hitching breath and pulled away enough to center his gaze on Dean's.

"I can figure out why *she* agreed to it, but why did you?"

Dean tasted Jacob on his lips but didn't go in for another kiss. He shrugged. "Because she thought I couldn't."

"Ah." Jacob tilted his head. "Well, I guess

you can't let her get away with assuming that just because you like cock that makes you, oh, I dunno, GAY or anything."

"Hey!" Dean didn't like the insinuation, especially since Jacob didn't know him well enough to judge him that way. "She knows I'm queer. I never pretended otherwise."

Jacob gave an exaggerated shrug and made a face. "You don't have to prove anything to me, sugar. Just wondering if you need to prove it to yourself or something."

"I've known I was queer since the eighth grade," Dean said flatly.

Jacob's gaze dropped to Dean's crotch. "Uh-huh. Like I said. You don't have to prove it to me. I had your dick in my mouth this morning, remember? Then again…"

"Then again, what?" Dean looked at the door, thinking how he should've walked out on this conversation ten minutes ago but hadn't, and not quite willing to ponder why.

"Even straight guys can be convinced getting head from another dude isn't gay." Jacob grinned, showing white teeth just a tiny bit too crooked.

Dean snorted lightly. "Yeah? The fuck you getting at, Jacob? You want me to suck your cock?"

Jacob rubbed at his crotch without breaking the gaze. He knew just how to work this, that little bastard. He'd known Dean all of two weeks and already had his number. Not that Dean was going to admit it, hell no. No guy got under his skin, not that he'd let on. Ever.

"Sure," Jacob said with a raised brow.

In answer, Dean grabbed Jacob's belt. Undid the buckle. Then the zipper. He freed Jacob's dick, stroking it from half-hard to full-on wood in half a minute after that. Jacob swallowed hard, eyes getting heavy-lidded.

"You think I don't suck cock?" Dean breathed, voice husky in anticipation.

"Well," Jacob said, feigning a nonchalance made obviously false by the tremor in his tone, "you haven't sucked mine."

Dean laughed at that, still stroking until Jacob pushed his hips forward. "Your spaghetti's going to get cold."

"I...like...cold spaghetti." Jacob's voice broke on a gasp, and that was all the impetus Dean needed.

He went to his knees and yanked down Jacob's jeans at the same time, baring the other man's body and gripping his tight ass. Jacob's cock was thick and hard, bobbing upward at the release from tight denim. Dean captured it at the base with one fist. His mouth found it next, and he slid Jacob's cock deep into the back of his throat.

Dean closed his eyes.

Not because he didn't want to see what he was doing. He liked watching, as a matter of fucking fact, but this was different. On his knees, giving head, was different than looking down at someone in the same place. On his knees, Dean liked to lose himself in the smells and sounds, the taste of whoever he was fucking. He let go of Jacob's ass to put Jacob's hand on the back of his head, curling Jacob's fingers into his hair. Urging him to guide the pace, if he wanted.

Yeah, Dean liked being on top. Fucking. But he wasn't averse to giving pleasure, either, and it was always, always better when the other person felt comfortable enough to say what they liked. Or show him. Dean wasn't above admitting he could be an asshole, but never let it be said he was a selfish lover.

"Fuck." Jacob's fingers tightened in Dean's hair and his hips pumped. "Fuck, baby, that's so fucking good."

Baby?

Dean paused at the endearment, his fist sliding up to meet his lips as his mouth came down.

Jacob didn't stop moving, fucking into Dean's hand and mouth. And after the barest moment, Dean went on. Sex talk didn't mean anything.

Then it didn't matter what Jacob said, because Dean unzipped his own jeans and pulled his cock free. Now came the complicated dance of hands and mouth, stroking and sucking at the same time. He had to catch up–Jacob was already making the low sound in the back of his throat Dean had come to recognize as his prelude to coming.

"Wait, wait." Jacob tugged harder on Dean's hair until Dean looked up.

It took Dean a second to understand Jacob wanted him to stop. Who the fuck ever wanted him to stop when he was blowing him? Dean looked up, one fist still pumping Jacob's dick, the other his own. "What?"

"I just…want…" Jacob licked his lips and swallowed, then cupped Dean's cheek. "Stand up."

Dean did with a quizzical laugh. Two men, pants around their ankles, cocks hard. His laugh slid into a groan when Jacob pulled him by the back of the neck to kiss him. It was a hard kiss, but not punishing. Jacob sucked Dean's tongue as his hand curled around Dean's dick.

"Use your hand on me," Jacob said as he stroked. "I want to make you come. I want your mouth on mine when you come all over my hand."

This was not what Dean had expected but fuck, Jacob was jerking him just right and the kiss went on and on, getting hotter by the second. Nothing to do but stroke Jacob's cock, too. They fell into mutual rhythm.

His balls got heavy, his cock impossibly harder. The kiss stuttered and broke as Jacob gasped. Dean didn't have the breath to gasp. He was going to come....

Jacob came first. Heat and slickness filled Dean's palm. Pleasure exploded out of him. He found the breath to groan.

Panting, Jacob kissed him again. Soft, this time. He still cupped Dean's cock, but his other hand came up to hold the back of Dean's neck. Forehead to forehead, he smiled.

"Hey."

"Hey," Dean said.

Jacob looked between them. "That was hot."

Dean laughed, shaking his head. "It was definitely not what I was expecting when you told me you wanted me to suck you off."

Jacob reached behind him to grab up a dish

towel, wiping his hands and handing it to Dean. "Baby, I am *not* what you are expecting."

Dean wiped his hands and put himself back in his jeans before stepping back. "Is that so?"

Jacob licked his forefinger and drew a "one" in the air. "That. Is so."

It was a good cue to leave. After all, they'd both already gotten off. Dean's stomach was rumbling, but dinner was cold and he could pick up something on the way home. He'd already spent last night with this guy. And the morning.

Jacob looked over his shoulder at the sink and the pot with the now-cold pasta. "This will only take a minute to warm up. You staying?"

Dean leaned to kiss him, relishing the taste of salt and beer on Jacob's mouth. "Sure."

Late-night conversations. Katie loved them. Darkness and distance provided by the phone made intimacy, and she loved that, too.

Jimmy was good at late-night talk. Jimmy had a voice like melting butter, all warm and soft and sweet. Rich. It didn't matter what he was saying, really. He told stories like some men built houses, layer by layer and piece by piece, until Katie realized hours had passed and dawn was breaking.

He'd make love like that, too.

Katie wondered if she'd ever find out. She'd met Jimmy weeks ago. He'd flirted with her right away. Asked for her number. He'd actually called, too, something that had surprised her since guys like Jimmy always said they'd call but never did.

Katie wasn't sure just how they'd fallen into late-night discussions about old movies, art, books, music. About their favorite colors and foods. All she knew was that she told Jimmy things she hadn't told any guy in a long time, and nothing she said ever seemed to put him off or be too much. Katie had spilled her guts about a lot of things from her most embarrassing moment to her secret fetish for knitted slippers.

They had become friends, and that was great, but Katie was beginning to wonder if that's all it would ever be.

"You stand in front of three doors," Jimmy said. "What color are they, what is behind each, and which do you pick?"

Katie laughed. "Where do you come up with these?"

"I have a book. Two hundred and seven of the most obscure questions to ask a beautiful woman."

At least he'd said she was beautiful. Katie

cleared her throat. "Let me think about it. You go first."

"That's not fair. I've had time to think about it longer than you have."

"Tell me anyway," Katie told him and settled deeper into the blankets.

"The doors are red, blue and purple. I pick the blue one."

"Why?"

"Because," Jimmy said, "blue's your favorite color and I bet you're behind it."

Heat twisted through her. "And what about the other doors?"

"I don't open them," Jimmy told her, "so I have no idea what's behind them."

"Good answer."

"Your turn."

Katie couldn't begin to think about doors and colors and what was behind them. Or rather, she could think, but every door she imagined was glass, each had Jimmy behind it, and no matter how hard she tried, she could open none of them. She sighed. "Tell me something else, Jimmy."

"Like what?"

"What's your favorite poem? Do you have one?"

Jimmy laughed softly, and Katie imagined the

brush of his breath against her neck. "Unless you count Jim Morrison lyrics as a poem, no, I guess I don't. What's yours?"

"I like e.e. cummings. My favorite starts off 'the boys I mean are not refined.'" Katie thought of the girls who bucked and bite, the boys who shake the mountains when they dance. She recited it to him from memory, and Jimmy was quiet for a moment after that.

"I never liked poetry," he said. "I had a…teacher…in school who made me recite lots of poetry. It was a way to…well, it doesn't matter why. I hated poetry because of that teacher. I never thought I could actually like a poem. But I like that one."

She heard him yawn and frowned, safe in knowing he couldn't see her. She was already making a face in anticipation of him ending the conversation, but her voice was neutral in reply when he told her he had to hang up.

"Yeah," Katie said. "It's late."

The invitation was on the tip of her tongue, but she bit it back. She didn't want to invite him out, not even to the coffee shop where they'd first met. He might say no. Worse, he might stop calling her.

"Night, Katie. Sleep tight."

"You too," Katie said and clutched the phone tight in her fingers after he'd disconnected before she did, too.

She was still thinking of that conversation when she got home with Dean in tow.

"Maybe that's your problem," Dean said as he flipped through a magazine she'd left on her coffee table. He tossed it down and looked at her. "What? Maybe he knows too much about you already. Destroyed the mystery."

"So then why does he keep calling me?" Katie nudged off one shoe with a sigh and then the other before flopping onto her couch. "Do men often call women late at night just to chat because they long to hear the sound of another voice? I think not."

"You're asking the wrong guy about that."

"Do you ever call *someone* late at night just to hear them talk?"

"Only if I'm jerking off at the same time," Dean said.

Katie made a face and wriggled her toes, free of the high-heeled pumps. "Maybe he's jerking off."

Dean shot her a grin. "Do you?"

"That," Katie said, "is none of your business."

Dean slid onto the couch beside her. "You do."

"Maybe. Once or twice." Katie curled her feet underneath her, looking at him. "He has a very sexy voice."

"So why not invite him over? Put on some soft music, make him dinner. Guys love that sort of shit." Dean tweaked her knee through her soft skirt. "Make the first move."

Katie shrugged. "I don't know. I like him. Maybe too much. I don't want to fuck it up, Dean. If he was into me like that, don't you think he'd have asked me on a real date or something instead of just calling me and talking for hours?"

"Maybe he's afraid, too. Guys can be afraid," Dean said.

"Are you?" She tilted her head to study him.

"I'm not afraid of anything." Dean frowned.

She let it go. She knew him better than that. After Ethan left, Dean hadn't said his name again. He'd erased Ethan from his life as thoroughly as though his lover had never existed as part of it. In some ways Katie admired that about Dean, his commitment to forgetting the past. On the other hand, she knew there had to be fond memories among the bad ones. She never regretted remembering relationships, even ones that ended.

So why was she so afraid to take a chance on one with Jimmy? Even if it didn't work out, she wouldn't have lost anything and might be missing something great. Katie sighed.

"Hey." Dean squeezed her again. "You're not having second thoughts, are you?"

"Huh? About Jimmy?"

"Focus," Dean said. He pulled out a strip of condoms from his back pocket and unfurled them, dangling, before tossing them onto the coffee table. "About us. This."

"Oh, the challenge." Katie drew out the word, then smiled. "No. I'm up for it."

Dean smiled too. "Good."

Katie was used to Dean encroaching on her personal space. He was a hugger, a toucher, a stroker. Working together on projects, bent over a computer screen, it wasn't uncommon for him to stand behind her with his chin on her shoulder to see what she was doing, or to put an arm over her shoulders while they walked someplace. Dean's physical affection was constant and casual.

This was going to be something totally different.

She wasn't sure what to expect when Dean kissed her. It was nothing like the New Year's Eve smooch. That had been rough and teasing, both of them a little drunk and laughing. Not serious.

She should've known better than to think her experience with that kiss could've prepared her for the sensation of Dean's mouth for real. He slanted his lips over hers as his hand came up to cup the back of her neck. The couch gave as he moved, dipping under his weight as he braced his hand on the back of it. His knee moved between hers. His mouth opened. He tasted of mint.

She'd closed her eyes automatically when he kissed her and opened them when he pulled back. Dean blinked, eyes heavy-lidded, mouth wet. He slid his tongue over his lips.

"That's a start," Katie said.

Dean laughed, low. "You're not going to give me one fucking inch, are you?"

"No. You're going to have to work for this, Dean." She moved closer and brushed his lips with hers back and forth before pausing a breath away. "I told you it wasn't going to be easy."

His fingers tightened at the base of her skull. When he licked his mouth again, his tongue teased her lips. They kissed again, deeper this time. Longer. When they pulled apart this time, Katie's heart had started up a determined thunder-thump she felt in all her pulse-points.

"Your mouth," Dean murmured, "is so soft."

She laughed and tipped her head back when he moved to kiss her jaw and throat. "All of me is soft."

Dean pressed his teeth to her skin and in the next moment, Katie felt sharp suction. His hands shifted, sliding down her body to her hips. She was on Dean's lap a moment after that, straddling him with her knees pressing the couch's soft cushions and her hands on his shoulders.

The kiss got harder still. Tongues tangling, teeth clashing, lips nipping. Dean gripped her hips. Katie pressed herself against him.

This was definitely working for her, but for Dean? Not so much, at least so far as Katie could tell from the lack of stiff, hard cock pressing against her. She broke the kiss and cupped his face in her hands.

"Close your eyes."

He narrowed them, but didn't close them. "Huh?"

She took his hand from her hip and put it to her breast, shifting his thumb to rub over her tightening nipple. "These are distracting you."

Dean looked at his palm full of breast and gave her a rueful grin. "Naw."

Katie laughed softly. "Close your eyes. Wait. I have a better idea."

She'd tied her hair back this morning with a soft vintage scarf. Now she pulled it off and unwound it, letting the silky fabric slide over her fingers. She folded it in half as Dean watching, eyes still narrowed.

"I didn't know you were kinky, Katie."

"Shh." She tied the scarf over his eyes and smoothed the fabric, letting her fingers trace his cheekbones and chin before running a fingertip over his lips. He tried to bite her finger but she pulled away before he could.

Then she kissed him again. They kissed for a long time without a break. Katie unbuttoned Dean's shirt and put her hand inside, flat on his bare chest. His heart had begun thumping, too. His cock had also gone satisfyingly hard against her crotch.

Still kissing him, she moved off his lap and unzipped his fly. Dean lifted his hips to help her push his pants over his hips. He wore navy boxer briefs, the front tenting impressively. Katie took his prick in her hand through the soft material of the briefs and stroked.

Dean groaned into her mouth.

If she spoke, it might spoil the illusion for him, whatever that might be. Whoever he was imagining. So Katie kept silent. Instead, she kissed and stroked him, eventually freeing him from the confines of his briefs. She couldn't help the small groan of her own when at last she held Dean's silky hot cock against her bare skin.

Katie'd been serious when she told Dean she had no doubts she could make him come. Now, with his prick in her hand and his mouth open beneath hers, begging, Katie was determined to enjoy it. And not just because it would mean she'd win this challenge.

She moved her mouth down his body, kissing and sucking gently on his smooth, warm skin. Sucking harder when Dean's breath caught and the tight muscles of his belly jumped beneath her lips. A great hand-job wasn't about showing off, in Katie's opinion. It was about paying attention.

It was also about being smart. With a quick glance at Dean, Katie reached for the bottle of lube she kept in the drawer of the end table. She filled her palm with thick, slippery fluid. This time when she stroked him, Dean muttered a low curse.

With this beautiful body in front of her, Katie

wanted to worship it. Take hours kissing and sucking and licking every curve and line. Her cunt ached, sweetly aroused at the erotic fantasies stroking Dean gave her. She'd never been a fan of denial, either, saw no point in it, so as she stroked Dean's cock a little faster, she also slid her hand into her panties and gently squeezed her clit between her thumb and forefinger.

She moved from Dean's lap to the couch without letting go of his erection. She leaned to kiss him and his greedy mouth took hers in a kiss deep and long and fierce. Her fingers in her panties moved faster as she jerked him off.

When Dean put his hand on hers, changing the pace, the pleasure building in her clit leaped up a notch. This was everything she loved about sex—a little fast, a little rough, a little furtive and dirty. Yet safe, too. Nothing would change between them because of this. Nothing really could.

"Fuck," Dean muttered as his hand gripped hers, moving it faster. "I'm gonna come...."

"Me too," Katie murmured as her fingers circled her clit faster.

Dean let out a short, startled gasp. Maybe at the sound of her voice, maybe at his orgasm. His cock throbbed in her fist and he shuddered. Heat spilled over her fingers and the scent of him, along with his low, desperate growl, sent Katie tipping over the edge right along with him.

His hand kept hers from moving more. Panting, Katie fell back against the couch cushions and took her hand out of her panties. Then she laughed, soft at first before getting slowly louder.

Dean hooked the scarf from his eyes and tossed it at her. "You cheated."

"I didn't cheat," she protested. "I told you I could get you off. I did."

Dean glanced at her lap, her skirt rucked up around her waist, and gave her a smug grin. "So did you."

"Ah," Katie said, leaning in to brush a sweet kiss against his mouth, "but you didn't do it for me. I did it myself. So it doesn't count, does it?"

"Cheater," Dean murmured against her mouth, but didn't pull away.

The kiss lingered. She was surprised. Surprised more by the look on his face when she finally pulled away to rearrange her clothes.

"What?" Katie asked. "Like I was going to leave myself high and dry?"

Dean reached for a handful of tissues from the box on the end table, and took care of cleanup before tucking himself back into his pants. "I call do-over."

"Do over?" Katie guffawed and got up, letting her skirt fall back down around her ankles as she headed for the kitchen. "You want something to drink?"

Dean caught up to her in the kitchen. He trapped her between his body and the counter as she reached for a glass. "I mean it, Katie."

She paused. "Dean, it's no big deal. Really."

"It's a big deal to me."

Before she could answer or protest, her cell rang. She recognized the ringtone. "That's Jimmy."

Dean frowned and stepped back. "Guess you'd better answer, then."

"Is this going to make trouble between us? Because I'd never have agreed to it if I knew that." Katie grabbed her phone but didn't answer it. The call went to voice mail and beeped while she waited for Dean's answer.

"No trouble. I'll see you at work tomorrow, okay?"

"Dean–"

"Hey," he said, frown erased by a classic, sunny Dean grin. "This isn't over, Katie. Don't worry, I'll let myself out. See you tomorrow."

Her phone beeped with a text message. Also from Jimmy. Katie looked at it, then at Dean, who was already waving goodbye as he ducked out the door. "Dean!"

But he was already gone.

It hadn't been the best hand-job he'd ever had, so why the hell couldn't he stop thinking about it? Her hands had been small and soft, her mouth soft and sweet, her curves sweet and lush. Katie was a gorgeous woman and he liked her. Being queer didn't mean he couldn't appreciate her attributes, but until she put the blindfold on, he hadn't been able to really get into what they were doing.

He was more determined than ever to prove her wrong.

"Your face is going to stay that way," Katie said serenely from behind him.

She was the one who'd brought the coffee today, two paper cups of it bearing the familiar logo of The Green Bean from down the street. She handed him one and sipped from her own. She looked fresh and bright-eyed, a habit that annoyed him most days but particularly on this one.

"You couldn't even see my face. My face is fucking fabulous," Dean said.

"Your eyes are squinty," she said in a low

voice as she passed him, like she was sharing a secret though there was nobody around to hear them. She bumped him with her hip.

He followed her into her office and closed the door. She looked up with a sigh and set her cup down. Dean didn't sit.

"We didn't even fuck," he told her.

"Oh, for heaven's sake. Are you still on that?" Katie flipped her fingers at him and leaned back in her chair.

"We *said* we were going to have sex."

"We did have sex. Sort of." Katie crossed her legs and her skirt rode up, giving him a flash of thigh and something that looked suspiciously like pink satin panties.

"I want to try again," he said.

He'd known Katie for a long time. She often had a witty comeback or a response as subtle and effective as a raised brow. He got her, that was the thing, and knew she understood him, too. It was what made them great partners and better friends. Now, though, he could read nothing on her face, nothing in her eyes.

"I don't think that's a good idea," Katie said after a minute.

"What? Why not?" He wasn't used to this, someone turning him down. That was a cliché and arrogant, but true. Mostly because Dean had a finely honed sense of who to hit on, not necessarily, as Katie had so often said, that nobody ever wanted to refuse him.

Dean had been refused before, all right. He knew how it felt. It sucked.

"Because we're friends, Dean, and I don't want to mess that up."

"You agreed to it before."

"That was before," Katie said calmly enough, but he didn't have to hear a tremor in her voice to see she was sort of upset. He could tell by the way she didn't drink her coffee.

"Hey. What's going on?" Dean slid into the chair across from her and moved forward, forcing her to uncross her legs so his knees could press hers. "Something up with that douchebag Jimmy or whatever the hell his name is?"

"Nothing's up with Jimmy. That's the problem."

"Forget him," Dean said. "If he can't see what's right in front of him…"

She laughed at that. "Right. Because you're the expert on seeing what's right in front of you?"

Dean frowned and stood. "The fuck's that supposed to mean?"

Katie shrugged and swiveled her chair back and forth. "Maybe I want more than a quick fuck from him, that's all."

"Isn't the problem you're not getting *any* sort of fuck?"

She sighed, her shoulders lifting and dropping with the force of it. "Forget it. You wouldn't understand."

"So…the challenge is off?"

Katie eyed him, one eye squinting and her head tilted as though she were seriously studying him as something foreign. Incomprehensible. "Why do you have such a bug up your ass about this sex thing?"

"You said I couldn't," Dean told her.

And that was the truth, mostly.

His phone rang, the ring tone a snippet of classical music he'd assigned to Jacob. His fingers slipped a little on the phone's glass face as he looked, anyway, to make sure that was the number. He didn't answer it.

Katie was smiling at him when he looked up, her smile half-quirked. "Was that him?"

"There is no *him*," Dean said.

Her grin got a little broader. "Right."

She swiveled again, kicking her foot up and down, showing off an expanse of shapely thigh he knew she'd never have revealed to any-one else in the office. Katie didn't do shit like that, use her tits and ass to get attention, even though she could. She was always more com-fortable with him than with the other men in the office, and for the first time, this stung a lit-tle.

"Is it because you don't think I'm manly enough?"

Her grin wavered, her brow furrowed. "What?"

"You don't think I'm manly enough," Dean said, convinced.

"Oh, Dean. Really? C'mon. You should know better than that."

Her scoffing didn't make him feel better, espe-cially when she turned her chair to face the com-puter, dismissing him. Dean spun her around to face him again. Katie looked as surprised as he felt.

"I want to do it," Dean said in a low voice.

Katie drew in a breath. She smelled good. She always did, but today he seemed to notice it more. He seemed to notice everything about her more than usual today, most of it accompanied by the memory of her hand on his cock.

"Would it change your mind," Katie murmured, her gaze bright, her voice throaty, "if I told you I absolutely believed you could make me come?"

"I'll prove it to you."

Her laugh this time snagged, rough and sultry. He'd never heard her sound that way before. "Fine. Prove it to me if it's so important to you."

"Done," Dean said as his phone rang again, the same bit of classical music. "When?"

"Tonight? There's no point in waiting."

"Your place?"

"Be there at eight," Katie said. "I don't want to be up all night."

"Oh, you'll be up all right," Dean said. "Maybe until tomorrow morning."

It was no big thing, Katie told herself. It wasn't like she'd never thought about what Dean would be like in bed, or that she'd never gone to bed with a friend before. As a matter of fact, a few years ago she'd had quite a successful "friends-with-benefits" experience with a man she still kept in touch with, unlike many of her friends who'd tried that sexual experiment and had it end badly. So it was no big thing, but she couldn't stop thinking about it. How he'd smell

and taste and feel, if he could indeed get her off
the way he promised.

Katie was sure hoping he could.

Distracted by thoughts of Dean's hard cock,
she nearly got hit in the face by the door to the
coffee shop as she was heading in and someone was heading out. An old woman, layered in
scarves and carrying a monstrously large cup of
coffee, barely even looked Katie's way as she
pushed through the door, but fortunately instead
of clipping her face on the glass, Katie only
banged her elbow.

"Excuse you," she muttered, turning to watch
the woman pass.

It was the only reason she looked to the street
corner and saw Jimmy, wearing familiar and
delectable denim jeans, his longish hair tousled,
his face scruffy. He was leaning against the street
sign talking on a cell phone. If it had been anyone else, even an ex-boyfriend, Katie would've
had not even a second's hesitation in approaching
him. But this was Jimmy, master of the late-night
phone call. Things were always different in day-
light.

She didn't have time to scoot inside the coffee
shop before Jimmy looked up, still talking, eyes
getting bright. He smiled and said something that

must've been goodbye, because he slipped the phone into his front pocket and headed toward her.

"Katie."

"Hi, Jimmy." She sounded too breathy, too gooey, too junior high. Katie tried again. "How's it going?"

"Good, good." He nodded. The breeze moved his shaggy hair, and the sunlight lit up his face. He had eyes the color of caramel, something she hadn't remembered. "You going in?"

She glanced over her shoulder. "Oh. Yes."

"Good." Jimmy grinned again and held open the door, then followed her.

It was the same coffee shop where they'd met, but this time, Jimmy bought her latte and brownies for both of them. He pulled out her chair, too, something no man had done for Katie in a long time. Sitting across from him, their knees bumping every so often, Katie tried hard not to think of this as anything romantic.

It was hard, though, with Jimmy keeping eye contact and laughing at her jokes. Or at the way he casually brushed past her on the way to get more napkins, some cream for his coffee, a fork. He touched her, hand flat on her back between her shoulder blades as he passed. And on the upper arm, and on the shoulder when he got up to greet another friend who'd come into the shop.

He touched her seven times, never in any way that could've been construed as anything more than casual, but Katie counted each time, her nerves tingling more with every press of his palm against her. By the time she'd finished her coffee, the brownie not even touched as she'd lost the capability to eat anything while Jimmy flirted with her, Katie thought if he touched her again she was going to melt into a puddle right then and there.

"Well, hey, it's been great," Jimmy said suddenly with a glance at the clock on the wall behind her, "but I have to scram."

He stood, leaving Katie blinking and thinking of something witty to say, but he'd already squeezed her shoulder again and was pushing in his chair.

Damn.

He'd reduced her to speechlessness, which was not her normal state at all. She really hated not being herself around him, that somehow he'd made her the sort of woman who got all giddy and dumbstruck with crush. More than that, though, she hated that Jimmy seemed either oblivious to his effect on her, or so used to creating that response in women that he took it for granted.

"Thanks for the coffee." Katie stood, too.

"Any time. I'll call you," Jimmy promised and shot her a grin.

Katie watched him go, wishing she could believe his offer was real and for her, instead of just his standard response to every female in the world.

Jacob hadn't been too happy that Dean was going to Katie's tonight. If any other man had snapped at Dean like that, told him off, said he'd better get his priorities straight instead of fucking around just because he "could" and not because he "should," well, Dean would've told him to fuck off. It had come close to that, actually.

"You want me to cancel?" he'd asked, still tasting garlic and red sauce and wishing Jacob had brought all this up before they'd started eating.

Jacob had cocked his head and looked Dean up and down with a flat, cold gaze. "Would you, if I asked?"

"No."

Jacob had shrugged. "Then do whatever the hell you want to, Dean. I won't be that guy."

"What guy?" Dean had asked, though he was pretty sure he knew.

"The one," Jacob said as he got up and took his plate, food uneaten, to the garbage can to scrape it, "who waits around for you to figure everything you want and need is right in front of you, while you just keep walking away."

"Is that a threat?"

Jacob had shrugged and given him another long look. "No, baby. It's a fact."

Then he'd pointed at the door, and Dean had gone with his tail between his legs, a fact that pissed him off so much he thought he might just delete that little prick from his phone entirely. But he didn't. Sitting here in the car in front of Katie's house, Dean held the phone and waited for it to ring.

But it didn't.

The last guy he'd wanted and needed had cheated on him, lied to him and finally, left him. What still hurt wasn't that Ethan had fucked around and been dishonest about it, but that in the end Dean had forgiven him and Ethan had still walked away.

The one who waits around for you to figure everything you want and need is right in front of you, while you just keep walking away.

"Fuck that," Dean said aloud and tossed the phone into his glove compartment so he wouldn't hear it not ringing. He looked at the house and wet his lips with his tongue.

He was going to do this, all right. The reasons had gone blurry–he was sure Katie would be okay if he cancelled, but then she'd always look at him when she thought he wasn't looking and think about how he'd been a pussy. Hell, did that even matter? Why had this become so important? Why couldn't he just let it go?

The porch light blinked twice. Katie. He probably looked like the biggest douche ever, sitting here in the car like he couldn't make up his mind. Dean drew in a breath. In, out. Game time.

She greeted him at the door with a smile that didn't quite reach her eyes. "Hey. I thought you weren't going to make it."

"No. I'm here." He paused, suddenly feeling like maybe he should've brought flowers or something like that. Feeling lame. This was Katie, for fuck's sake, his friend. He could've at least brought a bottle of wine.

"C'mon in." She stepped aside and closed the door behind him.

They stood in the entryway, more awkward than they'd ever been with each other. Dean remembered his senior prom, standing with his date and feeling the same way. Feeling like he was putting on a show that wasn't fooling anyone.

Should he kiss her? He'd have kissed her on the cheek or hugged her, at least, if they hadn't agreed to fuck. He'd have at least slipped an arm around her waist as he followed her to the living room to give her a squeeze as he asked about her day. All things he'd done before but now couldn't quite manage.

"Something to drink? I have some of that wine you like," Katie offered. "Actually, I already poured it, so you'd better be having some. I can't finish the bottle myself."

She pointed to the coffee table. Bottle, two glasses. It was his favorite.

"Yeah." Dean sat, took a glass, looked at her. "Do you need this?"

Katie looked a little surprised as she sat next to him, reaching for her own glass. "You mean…for tonight?"

"Yeah." Dean cleared his throat. "You want to back out? Or you need to be a little drunk?"

Katie laughed and shook her head. "No, sweetie, I totally do not need to be a little drunk to fuck you. Unless…you don't want to?"

She looked wary and hesitant, an expression Dean felt on his own face and didn't like. "No. I mean…unless *you* don't want to."

Katie sighed heavily and sank into the couch cushions while sipping the wine. "Oh, Dean. Listen, this was your idea, so if you don't want to, I totally get it. We don't have to have sex. Believe me," she added somewhat sourly. "You won't be the first man today who didn't want to make love to me."

That sounded bad. Maybe even worse than his own trials with Jacob. Dean turned to face her. "That fucker Jimmy?"

She shrugged and ran a fingertip around the top of the wineglass, making it sing. "I saw him today. I mean actually saw, not talked to on the phone."

She detailed how they'd met by accident. The coffee, the touching. It pissed Dean off to hear how sad she sounded about it.

"He's a fucking moron," Dean said flatly. "A foron. Really, babe."

Katie's sigh was shaky as she put her glass on the table. "I should just forget him."

To his alarm, because Katie wasn't a wilting flower at all, Dean saw she was on the verge of tears. "Hey. C'mere."

He pulled her close so she could snuggle in at his side, her cheek to his chest. She fit just right in the curve of his arm, his chin against her hair. She sighed heavily again and put her arms around him.

"I'll be fine," she assured him, voice muffled.

He stroked a hand down her hair and they sat that way in silence for a few minutes. The words that came out of him next surprised him, quiet though he said them. "He wants to be in a real relationship with me."

"Of course he does," Katie said, brushing her cheek against his chest again. "You're fabulous."

"...no. I mean...yes," Dean said. "But that's not what I mean."

More silence.

"You're afraid," Katie said softly. "I get it. I know about you and Ethan, remember?"

For the first time in a long time, Dean didn't stiffen at the other man's name. For the first time, Ethan's face had faded enough another face could replace it. "I don't want to be like him, Katie, and that's what Jacob said I was like."

She looked up at him, her eyes wet though her cheeks were dry. "He said that?"

"Not exactly," Dean admitted. "I mean, fuck,

he doesn't know about Ethan. Not like you do. But he said he wasn't going to wait around while I just keep walking away."

"Ah." She didn't move away from him. "Well, sweetie, maybe he has a point, you know?"

"I don't want him to have a point," Dean said.

She smiled sadly, her mouth quivering. "We're a pair, aren't we? You've got someone you're not sure you want, I have someone who doesn't seem to want me."

To her chagrin, because Dean didn't want to be the reason Katie cried, her tears spilled over her lower lids and traced their way down her face.

"Hey," he said. "Don't, okay?"

He swiped the tear with the pad of his thumb and Katie shuddered, turning her face to press her mouth to his palm, holding his hand close to her face for a moment before looking up at him with still-sad eyes. A lot of women had cried on Dean's shoulder over the years, but Katie never had. Looking at her now, all he could think was how good a friend she'd always been, and how much he didn't want her to be unhappy.

She murmured against his mouth when he kissed her but made no protest. Her mouth opened. She tasted sweet, the way she had the other day. His hand went naturally around the back of her neck to cup it, her hair a soft, thick weight on his fingers. Somehow she ended up on his lap, straddling him, their kisses turning from soft and slow to hard and demanding.

She'd tricked him before, with the blindfold, but he didn't need it this time. His mind put together the taste and smell of her with the memory of pleasure, and his cock responded. He pulled her closer, kissed her deeper, put a hand on the small of her back to grind her down a little harder against his dick.

"Dean," she murmured into his mouth, but his kiss stopped her.

Dean favored men close to his size and build. Compared to that, Katie was so much smaller and softer, he had no trouble putting his hands under her ass and lifting her. She let out a small, strangled gasp but didn't stop kissing him. Their tongues twisted, tangling, and fuck, it felt good. Really good.

He didn't try to make it to the stairs, much less up them. Her rug was soft and thick and deep, and he laid her down on it, settling between her thighs as he closed his eyes and sank into the sensations. The semi-desperate surge of pleasure coiling in his gut surprised him, making him think his cock really did have a mind of its own.

Somehow she got him undressed, a feat he could only admire since they never stopped kissing and he was fumble-fingered about her clothes. In her bra and panties beneath him, Katie laughed softly as he tried to figure out how to unhook her bra and got it off herself.

"You really never have done this," she said.

"Of course not." Dean slid his hands up her sides but stopped just below her breasts to look into her eyes. "Did you think otherwise?"

She got up on her elbows to look at him. "I guess maybe I thought I wasn't that special."

"Shut your fucking mouth," Dean told her before kissing her again and saying against her lips, "you're special."

She laughed again into his kiss, and that was better than her tears had been. She lay back with him between her legs. Her hand found his dick and stroked it from half-hard to fully erect, and Dean shuddered at how good it felt. When she stroked her fingertips over his balls, he drew in a breath, holding it for a moment, before opening his eyes to look at her.

"Oh no," he said. "The challenge was to get you off."

"Sweetie, seeing you enjoy yourself goes a long way toward that."

Dean couldn't argue with that, since he was a fan of such tactics himself, but he shook his head. "I'm going to make you forget anyone else tonight, Katie. I promised."

"Already done," she breathed, eyes gleaming, and ran her hands up over his thighs. "Touch me."

He slid his hands up her sides again to cup her breasts. Her nipples tightened against his palms and she drew her lower lip between her teeth. She liked that, he thought, trying to imagine what a woman would like. The same things as a guy, probably if only he could figure out the right parts to focus on. If only he could find them, he thought as Katie parted her legs a little and arched her back.

Fuck, this might be harder than he'd thought.

He bent his mouth to a nipple, sucking gently. Not flat like a man's, Katie's nipple peaked and grew as he stroked it with his tongue. And wow, she bucked her hips up against his belly. Dean did the other nipple, too, until both of them were rosy red and hard.

Dean had seen plenty of hetero porn–his college roommate had been addicted to the stuff, leaving skin mags around and playing a nonstop collection of VHS tapes he rented from the video store. It had all seemed sort of vague and mysterious, unlike gay porn in which everyone had erections and came in great, spurting jets of jizz, on camera. Katie wasn't acting like a woman in a porn video. Aside from the lack of Lucite platform shoes, she was squirming only a little when he touched her.

Kissing her, though, was getting better and hotter. She pulled him to her mouth, her soft body wriggling under his. She was an amazing kisser, knowing when to pull back and when to suck his tongue just hard enough to get him moaning.

She shifted against his cock, hard on her belly, and ran a hand down his bare chest to tweak one of his nipples before pushing her panties down and wriggling until she got them off. She lay back, naked, her gaze bold but her chin lifted a little.

Dean wasn't stupid. "You're beautiful," he assured her.

She raised a brow.

He kissed her, hands stroking over her sides and hips, over her belly, then up again to cup her breasts so he could use his mouth on her nipples again. "You are."

"That feels good," Katie murmured, laying back onto the rug and running her hands through his hair.

It wasn't going to give her an orgasm, he knew that much. Dean might not like pussy, but he wasn't ignorant about anatomy. All those hours of trying to study while porn ran in the background might pay off now—at least he had an inkling of where to find her clit, something his college roommate never seemed to have managed if the sounds his girlfriends made in their bunk after lights out were any indication.

He rolled onto his side, kissing her mouth again, as his hand slid down her soft belly and through the tangle of curls covering her pussy. His fingers stroked down. This was utterly foreign, completely unexpected…and absolutely erotic for all that. She was soft and hot and wet, and when he found a small, hard bud with his fingertips, she cried out.

Bingo.

Katie opened her eyes. "Right there. That's good."

She put her hand on his wrist, shifting him a little, slowing his pace, but letting go as soon as he adjusted. Fascinated, Dean watched her sink back against the rug, her cheeks flushing as she closed her eyes. She bit her lower lip again before breathing in, lips parted.

This was so unlike anything he'd ever done. Cocks came in a lot of sizes, but they were all big enough to grip. To stroke. Beneath his fingertips was the one small spot he had to keep his attention on. This was the real challenge, and Dean wasn't going to fuck it up.

His cock ached, his balls heavy, as he stroked her, but he didn't move to do anything about it. He couldn't afford to lose track of what he was doing. Female orgasms, to his knowledge, could be tenuous and easily lost.

They kissed forever, and he didn't care. The longer they went, the better it got. He found a rhythm that turned out not to be so different than what he was used to, and the way Katie reacted–moaning softly, rocking her hips, he thought she was enjoying it.

She stiffened, her hand going to his wrist again, her mouth open beneath his but no longer kissing. "Oh…"

Dean paused, fearing he'd somehow done something wrong. "Katie?"

"Oh, god, so close," she whispered, and looked at him. "Just…slow down a little. Make it last."

Dean grinned, slowing his circling finger. "Like this?"

Her eyelids fluttered. "Oh, god…"

The sound of pleasure suffusing her voice sent a throb from the root of his cock all the way through it. She moved against his hand. The flush on her cheeks had spread down her throat, across her breasts, and without thinking too much about it, Dean bent to suck gently at her nipple again.

Katie cried out, something wordless and ecstatic. The feeling of her moving, the sound of her–fuck–the smell of her arousal sent slickness oozing from the head of his prick. His balls tightened. When she kissed him, he felt her clit pulse under his fingertips. She moaned into his mouth.

"Fuck me," Katie said, not like a command but more like a plea.

He wanted to, but there was the matter of logistics. Katie blinked again, her gaze clearing for a minute, and she pushed at him to roll him off her as she reached into the drawer of her end table to pull out a box of condoms. Just as she'd figured out how to get them both naked before he could, now she pushed him to sit up as she opened the box, tore open the package and sheathed him in latex before he could do more than shift his hips. Straddling him, her thighs gripping his, Katie put her hands on his shoulders. His cock rubbed at her belly and then lower as she looked at him.

"You sure about this, sweetie?"

"Did you come yet?" Dean asked, voice hoarse at the pressure of her cunt pushing his cock against his stomach. Her ass was smooth under his palms.

Katie smiled and reached between them to grip his dick at the base. She bit her lower lip, looking down, as she shifted and then…oh, fuck.

"Oh, fuck," Dean said aloud. "You're so hot. And tight."

Blinking, surprised, he let the pleasure wash over him as she sank onto his cock all the way. She was tight, and hot, and slick, too. Her cunt gripped him better than any fist ever had, and he had to breathe out, slowly, to keep himself from shooting off like a kid with his first strokebook.

Katie pressed her forehead to his shoulder for a second. "Oh. God."

He'd never fucked in this position before, but it didn't take him more than a second to figure out how to shift and thrust upward. His cock slid inside her without effort, and she bit down, hard, on his shoulder. Dean had never been one for painplay but that was too fucking much. His cock throbbed and he made a low, grinding noise.

"Yes," Katie breathed into his ear. "Fuck me. Just like that."

Soft, low, distinctly feminine, her voice was in no way like a man's. Her body, soft and curved, not like a man's. Nothing about this was like anything he'd ever even fantasized about, but Dean discovered it didn't fucking matter, not then, not with her cunt wrapped around his cock like that. Not with her tongue licking at the sore spot her teeth had left. Not with her moving on him, riding him. Fucking him as pleasure built and built and built.

"Touch me," Katie said into his ear. She took his hand, slid it between them, pressed his thumb to her clit. "Oh, yes. Right there. Like that, just like that…oh, god, Dean. Yes!"

Until this point, everything he'd promised her had been all talk. Until he felt her shudder and heard the soft sighing gasp of her breath as orgasm swept over her, Dean hadn't really been sure he could make her come. But now Katie rocked against him and his own climax shuddered through him. Perfect timing.

She blinked rapidly and looked at him, then

laughed. "Wow. Well, I guess I'd say you won. Very well done, sir."

Dean blew out a breath, fingers tightening on her hips as his breathing slowed. "Saying I told you so would make me sort of an asshole, wouldn't it?"

Katie kissed him lightly on the cheek and eased herself off him, stretching as she reached to snag up her panties and T-shirt. "Sort of."

He watched as she got dressed without appearing to be the least bit embarrassed. He admired that about her. Not that he was embarrassed, exactly. Just more like wondering what the hell he'd just done.

Katie looked over her shoulder at him as she pulled on her clothes, then frowned. "You all right?"

Dean nodded, sitting there on the floor with a condom on his getting-limp dick, after having fucked one of his best friends. A woman, at that. It wasn't his most shining moment.

But Katie, still frowning, crouched next to him and pulled over a small garbage can and handed him a box of tissues, then his clothes. "I didn't think you'd be the one to get all emo, afterwards."

"I'm not emo." Dean frowned and took care

of cleaning up, then pulled on his briefs and jeans.

Katie studied him. "Uh-huh."

"I'm not."

She smiled and stood on tiptoe to kiss his cheek again. "We fucked, Dean. And it was good. For me, anyway, and I'm pretty sure you enjoyed it. It doesn't make you straight. Just…open-minded."

Her smile urged his, even though none of this was as gratifying as he'd expected it to be. He'd thought it would feel like a conquest. Instead, he found himself hoping Jacob would forgive him.

"Damn it," he said, suddenly miserable. "Remind me that I like sort of being an asshole?"

"Why? Are you going to say you told me so?"

"No. Not about that."

She knew him too well, Katie did. "Ah. It's him, huh?"

"Jacob."

"*Him* has a name?" She looked impressed. "Wow, Dean. Wow."

"Fuck." He sank onto the couch and cradled his head in his hands. "Fuck, Katie, what did I just do?"

"Hey." She sat beside him and took his hand,

linking their fingers. "Seriously, you're going to give me a complex, here. What happened…do you really think it was all just that stupid challenge? I mean, I know you don't do pussy as a general rule, but…maybe that's why you did it. Not why you suggested it, sweetie–that was all your huge ego. But…maybe it's why you actually went through with it."

He wasn't getting it, and she could tell.

"What I mean is, being with him scares you. I know why. But being with me isn't scary. Right?"

"No. Of course not."

She smiled. "Because you and I both know that no matter how stellar that living room rug fuck just was, and it was pretty delicious, it's not going to lead to anything. Right?"

He gave her a cautious nod. "Well…right."

"And for me," Katie said, "I really just needed someone who was into me. Even if only for an hour."

"I'm into you for longer than that," Dean told her and squeezed her hand.

She laughed, sounding better than she had earlier, which made Dean feel better. "You know what I mean."

"Yeah. I do." He leaned back against the couch

cushions and stared at the ceiling. "He makes it all seem so easy."

"It's not how he makes it seem," she said. "It's how he makes it feel."

Jacob made it all feel easy, too. Dean frowned as Katie's cell phone rang, vibrating the coffee table. She looked at it and sighed, but didn't pick it up.

"It's Jimmy."

"Douchebag," Dean said and picked it up. "Hello?"

"…Katie?"

"She's busy," Dean told the guy.

"Oh. Um, can I leave a message?"

"No," Dean said, and hung up.

"Dean!" Katie looked shocked, but was laughing.

Dean shrugged. "Maybe he'll think better of jerking you around."

"Maybe he'll never call me again!"

"Would that be a bad thing?" Dean asked. "For real?"

Katie frowned without answering, and Dean pulled her close to hug her. They sat like that for a while without speaking. Then she sighed and pushed away from him.

"Go to him," Katie said.

Dean nodded and stood, then handed her the cell phone. "Call him back."

Katie almost bailed.

She'd waited until the morning to call Jimmy, not sure if she wanted to go down that road, maybe waiting to see if he'd call her first. He didn't. She wasn't sure how she felt about that.

It didn't matter how she felt now, though, since she'd already called him and asked him to meet her for coffee. He'd hesitated before saying yes, a pause that had lasted a thousand years while she forgot to breathe. She wasn't, in fact, sure she remembered to now when he walked through the door.

He looked too damned good, she thought. It wasn't fair.

"Hey," Jimmy said as he slid into the chair across from her with a cup of coffee he put on the table. He shook his shaggy hair out of his face and shrugged out of his coat. His grin was at half-wattage.

"Hi, Jimmy." Katie had a mug of coffee in front of her, but she hadn't even sipped it. It was cold now, but she clutched it anyway as though the porcelain would warm her hands.

"This is nice. Meeting like this. Thanks for

asking me." Jimmy sounded hesitant, uncertain. Not his usual self at all.

But what was his usual self? Did Katie even know? She had to admit she probably didn't. Everything about Jimmy was late-night conversation, and just because she'd bared her soul to him didn't mean he'd done the same.

"Thanks for coming. It's nice to see you."

They never talked like this. Even the first time he'd called her, they'd slipped into a loose back-and-forth that had only gotten easier over time. Now it was as though they'd only just met and had no reason to get to know each other better.

Jimmy's smile amped up a notch, still far from his usual bright grin, but noticeable. "Yeah. Two times in one week, that's some kind of crazy, huh?"

Katie had always believed honesty to be the best approach, but facing Jimmy across the tiny café table, all she could think of was how she wanted to make up some lame excuse for why she wanted to see him instead of just telling him the truth. "Yeah. Super crazy."

Jimmy seemed to relax a little bit, his long fingers turning his cup around and around on the table. His knee nudged hers. "Sorry."

"It's okay."

This was going nowhere. Katie hated it. She wanted to ask him if he liked her, or if she was just some myth, a story he liked to tell over the phone. She wanted to tell him about how she smiled at the sound of his voice. Of how she wanted more.

Jimmy glanced over her shoulder toward the counter. "I'm going to grab a refill. You want one?"

Katie shook her head. "No, I'm fine, thanks."

He touched her again as he passed. A hand on her shoulder, fingers curving and squeezing just momentarily. It was too much, the final straw, that casual touch that felt too good.

She got up without thinking, without looking back, heading out of the coffee shop and down the street. The wind burned her eyes, not tears, she told herself as her heels click-clacked on the sidewalk.

She was almost to the alley before he caught up to her.

"Katie!" Jimmy hooked her elbow, turning her as she stiffened at the sound of her name. He didn't let go. "Hey. Wait."

Katie opened her mouth to protest or maybe just to walk away without a word, she wasn't sure and had no time to decide before Jimmy was kissing her. Openmouthed and hungry, his hands on her hips pulling her close up against him. He tasted better than she'd imagined, his kiss deeper, his body harder.

He pulled away, shoulders rising and falling with his breath. His gaze searched hers. "I didn't…was that…"

Katie kissed him. Softer than he'd done, her tongue stroking his as her fingers wound in the hair at the back of his neck. She pulled a little as his hands gripped tighter on her hips. She felt the bulge of his crotch through denim against her belly, and she pulled away, her own breath coming fast and sharp.

Jimmy smiled, his lips wet. "I should've done this a long time ago."

"Why didn't you?"

"I wasn't sure you wanted something like this," he said. "With me, I mean."

People passed them on the street, some giving them curious glances but most ignoring them. He stepped her backward into the relative privacy of the alley and leaned against the brick wall of the storefront without letting her go. Katie pressed against him, noticing he'd run out after her without a coat.

"Why on earth not?" she cried, pushing at him with her fists but not too hard. "God, Jimmy. We've been talking for months. You know the color of my favorite panties and the name of my first dog!"

"I know, I know, but...hell, I'm better on the phone than in person," he said.

Katie frowned and swiped her tongue over the taste of him lingering on her lips. "That sounds like a very bad excuse."

He sighed, looking serious. "I know. B-but..." Jimmy paused, drew a breath. "Well, I'll tell you. Until I was about fifteen, I stuttered."

Katie raised a brow.

"I grew out of it, or taught myself not to, whatever," Jimmy said slowly. "But by then I'd already found out I was better on the phone than talking to someone face to face. On the phone I could take my time or something, I don't know. It became a habit."

She shook her head. "I don't care if you stutter. You could've told me."

Jimmy nudged her just a bit closer into the space between one cocked leg and the opposite thigh. "I liked you the first time I met you, Katie. But then we started talking..."

"And you didn't like me any more?"

"No." He laughed. "I liked you more. A lot more. I didn't want to ruin it."

She made a disgruntled noise, already forgiving him because to do anything else would only spite herself. "You almost did."

"I know. I'm sorry." Jimmy kissed her again, lingering this time. "Do you think we could start over?"

"Hell no," Katie told him, wrapping her arms around him and getting up on her toes to return the kiss. "Start at the beginning? No way. Let's go straight to third base. Unless," she paused meaningfully, "you really are better on the phone."

Jimmy grinned, eyes gleaming, and leaned in close to whisper in her ear. "Why don't we go to my place and you can decide for yourself?"

"That," Katie said, "sounds like an excellent idea."

Dean had brought flowers.

He didn't even know if Jacob liked flowers.

Dean liked flowers, purple and red and yellow, tied with a green ribbon. He liked them in vases around his house. Dean liked flowers because they were pretty and they didn't last long, and he didn't have to take care of them the way he'd have had to be responsible for a potted plant.

Maybe it was time he stopped being so afraid of taking care of things.

He'd just tossed them into the bushes by Jacob's front door when he was caught by the door opening. Jacob looked at the bushes. Then at Dean.

"Why are you throwing flowers into my bushes?"

Dean tried to look innocent and knew he failed by the way Jacob's eyebrows rose. "Uh…"

Jacob peered behind the bushes, then put a hand on his hip. "Did you bring me flowers and then throw them away?"

"Yes." Dean's jaw tensed.

Jacob smiled.

When Dean kissed him, it felt right. Like coming home. When Jacob kissed him back, it felt even better.

"I like flowers," Jacob said against Dean's mouth. "Thank you."

Dean pulled away just enough to look into Jacob's eyes. There was probably more to say but nothing came to him just then. He spoke with his body, his mouth using kisses instead of words to express what he wasn't sure he should say aloud. Jacob seemed to understand, though.

He smiled against Dean's mouth. "Come inside."

Dean nodded. Then he smiled too as he followed Jacob through the doorway, walking behind him.

Not walking away.

Under His Hand

By Anne Calhoun

After doing time at Fortune 500 companies on both coasts, **Anne Calhoun** landed in a flyover state, where she traded business casual for yoga pants and decided to write down all the lively story ideas that got her through years of monotonous corporate meetings. Her first book, LIBERATING LACEY won the EPIC Award for Best Contemporary Erotic Romance. Her story WHAT SHE NEEDS was chosen for Smart Bitch Sarah's Sizzling Book Club. Anne holds a BA in History and English, and an MA in American Studies from Columbia University. When she's not writing her hobbies include reading, knitting, and yoga. She lives in the Midwest with her family and singlehandedly supports her local Starbucks.

CHAPTER ONE

Tess Weston soaked a facecloth with cold water, then bent forward, drew her hair over one shoulder and held the cloth to the nape of her neck. Rivulets trickled down her back, merging with the sweat seeping from her pores. Even with the windows open, and a fan oscillating as languidly as a spoon through soup, the temperature on the second floor of her house was hotter than the ambient air outside.

She swiped the now-tepid cloth down her throat and paused at her collarbone. The washcloth soaked the thin ribbed fabric over her breasts while she considered the sheer curtains hanging lank beside the open window. Such an unremarkable thing, an open window, a simple pleasure people generally took for granted. Drew Norwood, her Navy SEAL boyfriend, had extensive experience managing risks of all shapes, sizes and situations. Given her borderline neighborhood, he'd weighed simple pleasures against physical safety and insisted on windows and doors locked tight at night. However, Drew had disappeared almost a month ago, as usual with no warning. Three times in the six months they'd been dating he'd simply vanished into thin air, reappearing weeks later sunburned, thinner and exhausted.

The disappearing act didn't bother her. It came with dating an active duty SEAL, and she was used to people walking out of her life. The reappearing, as abrupt and unannounced as the disappearing, still set her back on her heels.

Not much else did, but a brutal heat wave, an AC unit that had become a frankly ugly pile of scrap metal three days earlier, and no money for repairs, left her with two choices: sleep in a situation Drew adamantly opposed, or melt into a puddle in her bed. She preferred to dissolve into liquid bliss when he was the one heating her up, and she flat out didn't have the money to fix the AC.

What Drew didn't know wouldn't hurt him.

She scrubbed at her breastbone as if she could wipe away the disloyal thought, then draped the washcloth over the edge of the sink. When she shut off the bathroom light and stepped into the moonlight illuminating a path along the scratched hardwood floor, a shadow disengaged itself from the dark corner behind the bathroom door, clamped a hand around her wrist and spun her face-first into the wall. The callused palm clapped unceremoniously over her mouth muffled her instinctive shriek. With her free hand braced at shoulder height, and a strength born of sheer terror, she pushed back into an iron-hard body. Her captor didn't move an inch. Instead, he knocked her off balance by wedging one leg between hers, and with minimal effort forced her flat. He had superior size and strength, the advantage of surprise, and she was trapped.

Eyes wide with panic, she twisted her head and peered over the big hand engulfing the lower half of her face, but her vision only confirmed the input from the quivering nerves in her hypersensitive body. Heavy shoulders and a broad chest clad in black pinned her torso, and a ridged abdomen trapped the arm bent behind her back. Squirming futilely in an effort to regain her balance only ground her bottom against his hips, and her thin cotton bikini panties provided no protection from the insistent erection shoved firmly against her ass.

Knowing it was futile, she inhaled sharp and

hard, drawing breath to scream. The air rushing through her nose carried with it the familiar scent of musky skin and the sharp odor of no-frills soap used at Coronado. In a millisecond she plunged from ice-cold fear to weak-kneed relief, and sagged against the restraining body.

Drew. Back with no warning. In her bedroom, scaring her half to death.

But how?

She'd been working downstairs all night, the front and back doors secured with the handle lock and dead bolt. He had a key, but hadn't used it; the door would have caught on the chain. The downstairs windows were so warped that opening or closing one was a noisy process that took effort, even from Drew. But upstairs the windows were unlocked and slid, loose and flimsy, in their frames. Discarding the possibility he'd slithered under the front door, he must have clambered in through the damned open window in her bedroom.

"Tess, you are in so much trouble."

Silky menace simmered under the growled words as he shoved off his black stocking cap and tossed it behind him. His thick, sweat-dampened hair, bleached near-silver by hours in the sun and salt water, gleamed even in the midnight-blue of her bedroom. With a wickedly accurate sense of timing he'd caught her at her most vulnerable, dressed for bed in one of his tank undershirts, and string bikini panties. Her feet were bare, her body crushed between his and the wall, and she stood no chance of breaking free from his tight grip.

"I can explain," she said, but his palm muffled her words.

"What?"

The barked question told her that having the living daylights scared out of her hadn't atoned for her sin. She tossed her head back, away from his hand, and he lifted his palm just enough to let sound escape. "I said I can explain!"

His hand mashed down over her mouth again. "I don't want an explanation," he growled. "I've been gone for twenty-six days. I want *you*. Now."

A bolt of hot lust shot through her when his gorgeous tenor drawl, laced with rough need and tightly controlled ire, tumbled into her ear. She jumped when he nipped the sensitive rim of her lobe, then slapped her other hand up against the wall. Docile, trembling, she stood still for him as he pushed her panties down her thighs, then went to work on the buttons of his cargo pants. Sensations zinged through her as his abraded knuckles brushed against the soft, rounded flesh of her bottom. He made room for himself between her legs, the width of his thighs urging her feet farther apart, her thin panties straining against the muscles quivering in her legs.

Disconcerting, palpable desire streamed along nerves lit up by the adrenaline rush from his unorthodox appearance. Need coiled tight and hot between her thighs. Without conscious thought she arched her back and tilted her hips toward him.

His low, dry chuckle didn't mask the sound of a condom wrapper tearing. After a pause he settled big hands on her hips and lifted her up and forward, to the very tips of her toes. Turning her face to the side to rest her hot cheek on the cracked plaster, she closed her eyes as fear, the unintentional aphrodisiac, heightened the sensations swamping her. His rough black BDU pants chafing her inner thighs. The soft brush of his cotton T-shirt against her shoulder blades and back. Sweat slicking the skin of her bottom and his lower abdomen where he leaned into her. Whirling, sharp sparks settling low in her belly, ready for him to strike the tinder and set her on fire.

"Miss me?"

Did doubt linger under his taunting question? It was so hard to think with his hand pressed flat to her abdomen, his cock hot and hard against her bottom. Nuances aside, the answer flowed easily from her parted lips. "I always do," she whispered, and felt his breath hitch in response.

The eight-inch difference in their heights didn't deter him. He simply bent his knees, wrapped one arm around her waist to hold her up on her toes, and braced the other arm next to her face. His thick cock parted sensitive flesh only beginning to swell and dampen with arousal. He drove in, and she winced.

He went still. "You okay?" he asked, his voice roughened, strained.

No…maybe… "I…yes."

A soft, almost unwilling groan eased out of him, then he began to thrust, deep and hard. Experience had taught her that although the first time would be fast and furious, she could come from the intensity alone, riding the waves of Drew's weeks-long adrenaline rush. Sometimes they made it upstairs before he was buried deep inside her, but more often than not he had her up against the door or on her rickety kitchen table. Watching Drew drive into her body, then shudder in her arms, reduced her to *female* at its most primitive. Taken. Possessed. The spoils of battle, even. She would come under the sting of his teeth on her shoulder, the brutal grip of his hand on her hip.

Tonight was different. Tonight the remnants of shock entwined with lust in her veins, and she added *submissive* to the list of adjectives describing how she felt when he had her spread and penetrated within thirty seconds of walking in the door, or, as the case may be, climbing through the still-open window. The unorthodox position left her off balance, straining up on tiptoe with her forearms braced in front of her face, pushing back into each thrust to avoid smacking her forehead on the wall. Her helpless acceptance made him growl again, low and deep in his throat.

His strokes were relentless, almost punishing, as was his arm around her waist, clamped down on her slippery flesh. The fingers of his other hand gathered her loose, sweat-dampened waves of hair at her nape and turned her head to the side so he could look at her. Her eyelids fluttered, on their way to closing as desire surged with each slick stroke, but an unfamiliar tenseness flashed behind the familiar hot need in his blue eyes.

For a brief moment she surfaced from the

whirlpool of erotic sensation, but he angled his hips forward, stroking over a spot inside her that sent hot, electric pulses zinging through her. She succumbed to the immediate. The ribbed undershirt chafed her nipples each time they brushed the wall, and pleasure swelled in her clit. She shivered and moaned over the sound of his abdomen slapping against her ass.

With an inadvertent tug that made her gasp, his damp hand stroked down through her hair and across her rib cage to cup the top of her sex. One fingertip circled her taut, slick nub. She threw her head back, straining into his unmovable body as he maintained his pace, fast and hard. Her orgasm slammed into her a split second before he ground his hips against her bare bottom and gave a stuttering groan. His cock swelled and pulsed inside her convulsing channel as he mouthed her jaw and neck through slow, jerky orgasmic strokes. Then he exhaled against her shoulder, letting his weight slump into her body.

As the waves subsided she sagged in his grip, waiting for her jellylike muscles to firm up enough to hold her weight. When they did she tossed a languid smile over her shoulder, her needy gasps turning soft with satisfaction. That was beyond the heat of a normal welcome home fuck, well into incendiary, and surely sex that amazing negated the issue of the naughtily open windows.

He didn't smile back. A deep red flush stood high on his cheekbones, visible even under his perpetual tan. Sweat trickled through the blond stubble on his jaw. "I missed you, too, Tess. Now you can explain about the windows."

Oh shit.

He withdrew as he spoke. Given the hint of steel under his soft tone, she did *not* want to be naked for this conversation, so she pushed herself upright and yanked up her panties. The cotton resisted, clinging to her damp skin as she peered at his back, headed for the bathroom.

"Don't move." The words were tossed over his shoulder in a curt fashion that made her freeze.

Definitely a panties-up conversation.

When he came back into the bedroom he stopped in the same strip of moonlight she'd occupied when he'd ambushed her. His short blond hair lay plastered forward, serious stubble shadowed his jaw and the planes and curves of his face were expressionless in the pale swath of light as he considered her. She expected him to look at her body. Her tank—his tank, really—was soaked with water and sweat and therefore practically see-through, and her nipples pushed pertly against the material. Tiny white string bikini panties cut high on her hip covered her trimmed curls, and her legs were bare all the way to her painted toenails. Under normal circumstances his gaze would be all over her, but instead he focused intently on her face.

She twisted her hair into a loose knot at her nape, crossed her arms and stared right back. His black cargo pants were up and buttoned, his T-shirt plastered to his muscled torso. Bizarrely, he was barefoot. It was on the tip of her tongue to ask him where his boots were, but she bit back the question as irrelevant, given the currents swirling in the hot night. His first hours back were always dark and intense—whether from long-suppressed need or a sheer human desire to reestablish a connection, she didn't know or care. Usually by this point they were sharing a shower, but his distant demeanor felt like a bucket of ice water poured over her head.

After a solemn, purposeful glance at the windows, he looked back at her, his blue eyes glinting in the darkness. "What am I going to do with you?"

Tess kept quiet. He'd told her what he'd do if she slept with the windows open, but if he didn't remember, she wasn't giving him any hints.

He approached her with measured strides, his eyes never leaving her face. His palms closed hot and firm around her wrists, turned her and lifted her hands back to the wall, just above shoulder height. With a gentle tap of his bare foot against her ankle he urged her legs a little wider apart. Heat flamed in her cheeks as she bent forward, her ass tipped toward him. Having sex like this was one thing, but it was quite another to have a conversation with him at her back. This was a power play, a conscious and unsubtle one. Drew knew exactly what he did, and worse, how she'd respond.

"Didn't we just do this? And what the *hell* were you thinking to scare me like that?" she asked, nerves stiffening her spine, vertebra by vertebra.

He didn't answer, and if he wanted to avoid a fight about the windows, he'd gone about it the wrong way. She drew breath to lay into him, but when he shifted between her spread legs and laid his warm, damp chest along her spine, she softened back into the sensual aftermath. His movements calm and easy, he gathered her hair in one hand and sent it cascading in dark waves over her left shoulder.

"Your hair was pink when I left."

Okay, she could talk about her hair. "I felt like a change," she said, breathless and again off balance.

He braced his hands just outside of hers, bent his head and pressed a kiss into her right shoulder, making his torturously slow way to her neck before nudging her head to the side and kissing along the soft skin under her jaw. Each openmouthed kiss, the only point of contact between his body and hers, resonated in her hard nipples and, more potently, in her still-eager clit.

"How long do you think it took me to climb up on the porch roof, open the window and get in here?"

Dammit. She wasn't going to be able to duck this or make it up to him the old-fashioned way. Worse for her, one hard, fast fuck hadn't been enough—not in her sultry, stifling bedroom, not after twenty-six days without him, not after the scare of her life—so distracting heat licked at her skin while she tried to estimate how long she'd been in the bathroom, brushing her teeth. Thirty seconds? The American Dental Association recommended brushing for two minutes, twice a day, but she never lasted that long. She gave up and split the difference. "A minute?"

He set his teeth against her slick shoulder before replying. "Ten seconds, Tess. Ten seconds to pull myself up onto the roof, walk across the peak, open the screen and climb in. It takes longer to describe it than to do it. You didn't even see me when you came into the bedroom."

"You were already in the room when I came up? I didn't hear anything," she said, peering over her shoulder.

He met her eyes without expression. "One, opening a screen doesn't make much noise. Any kid who's snuck out of a house could do it. Two, as loud as you were playing Nickelback you wouldn't have heard an M-16 firing. Not safe, Tess. Not safe at all."

Sheer embarrassment heated her cheeks and closed her eyes as she turned back to the wall. She'd had "Far Away" on repeat for over an hour, ostensibly for background noise as she sketched versions of an ornate spiral staircase destined for a downtown loft. The developer knew her earlier work and asked for designs; if she got the commission, she'd create twenty unique staircases and add to her growing reputation for custom work. The payment would buy a new

HVAC system, and put a little extra in the bank. But between Drew's prolonged absence and the vulnerability in the song, the pages were half sketches of intricate decorative work, half rough drawings of his face in ten different attitudes.

With a firm but gentle grip he turned her head to the corner, still hung in dark shadows. "I watched you. You took off that sexy skirt I love and put on this undershirt," he said. Her belly jumped as he fingered the hem of the tight white tank he wore under his uniform. "Then you made the bed just so you could get in it, brushed your teeth, and tried to cool off with that wet cloth. Water trickled down your neck and over your breasts, Tess."

He drew a deep breath, and she took the moment of respite from his hot, hard voice to try and slow her pounding heart. He'd been close, less than two feet from her. Watching her, getting hard for her. The images were flat-out carnal, but what if someone other than Drew had been hidden in the corner?

Despite the heat, goose bumps shimmered over her skin. "I see your point."

"Do you? Put yourself in my place and then tell me you see my point."

He was taut against her back, biceps bulging

in the deceptively lean arms braced on either side of her face, and she tried to imagine the scene from his perspective. Driving up her street after a month away, exhausted, hungry for sex and food and comfort, in that order, eager to see her, but finding the windows open late at night when he'd specifically told her it was too dangerous. But what was his *place*?

He was her boyfriend, which could mean a great deal, or not much at all. He took her out to eat. She packed picnic lunches for days at the beach. They went to street fairs and outdoor concerts and the movies. He slept at her house when he could. She kept him apprised of her ever-changing work schedule. They were exclusive and had been for six months, but when did exclusivity go from *I won't see anyone else* to *I accept your right to make demands of me*?

She went rigid at the thought of such dangerous intimacies. "Do you want to hear my side of the story?"

Smart, smart Drew knew all too well how to handle her. Only when he'd gently pulled her back against him and licked a delicate path along the rim of her ear, then down to her soft earlobe, did he whisper, "I'm listening."

"The air conditioner broke last week."

She owned her aging house, a tiny, slightly off-kilter two-story painted a fading, funky shade of lavender unremarkable for the eclectic neighborhood near her studio space in the warehouse district. "Eclectic" meant affordable prices for interesting-if-dilapidated architecture, and diverse, opinionated neighbors who were passionate about the neighborhood, its causes and people. It also meant she walked home from her studio past addicts, dealers and drunks, hookers and pimps, homeless families and groups of aimless young men. Break-ins were frequent. After one weekend with her, Drew was already on friendly terms with her neighbor, Mrs. Delgado, given his polite manners and Southern drawl. But with his well-honed sense for trouble, he'd recognized the neighborhood's good and bad elements and formed a decidedly negative opinion about her ancient air conditioner and the windows.

"I figured as much," he said, his voice dry.

"And you still scared the daylights out of me?"

He ignored her question, or at least she thought he did. "Why didn't you get it fixed?"

She threw a glare over her shoulder. "I need to pick up extra shifts at The Blue Dog to come up with the money."

"How much?"

"More than I have until I work the extra shifts."

"You said they were overstaffed and tips were down. How much, Tess?"

This relentless Drew was new to her, as if a stranger had come home in her boyfriend's body. "Six hundred dollars," she said, knowing he wouldn't like the answer.

His teeth ground, then he shifted his weight behind her. "I left money for you."

This was true. He'd tried to give her a thousand dollars in twenties, and the names of two navy buddies she could call day or night, for any reason, when he was gone. She'd refused both. A short, tense "discussion" ensued, one she'd thought she'd won when he stuffed the neatly rolled money into the pocket of his cargo shorts. She'd turned her back on him for less than a minute to retrieve his wallet from her nightstand. On his way back to the base he'd called to inform her that in the sixty seconds she'd left him alone in her kitchen, he'd put the cash in an empty Folgers Instant can at the back of her narrow pantry and the phone numbers in her cell phone. The next day he'd left on his most recent mission.

She had no intention of using the phone numbers, let alone the money.

"This is my life, Drew, not an emergency. I won't take your money. If I used it I'd need months to earn enough to pay you back, and besides…"

Her voice trailed off when his head dropped forward to rest on her shoulder.

"You don't have to pay me back."

"I do." This was important, although for reasons that grew hazier with each passing day.

There was a pause while his even breaths merged with the sweat trickling down her back. "Tess," he said, his voice totally without heat, "what do I have to do to earn your trust? Because I can't keep going like this."

The words, their empty tone, sent a shiver down her spine. She pulled her hands free of his and spun to face him. "You can trust someone and not take money from them, Drew!"

"You think I'm going to count up favors and make you work them off on your back?"

Her eyes widened at his crass question. "Of course not!"

He kept his arms on either side of her head while his blue eyes, somehow both sad and curious, searched hers. "Because it's not just the money. For all practical purposes I live here, and yeah, I buy groceries or fix things around the house, but it's a dirt-in-the-eyes, bare-knuckles street fight to get you to take anything I offer. You work harder than just about anyone I know, but half the time I come over here and you've got four cans of corn in the cupboard and nothing in the fridge. Christ, you won't use six hundred dollars to be safe, not to mention comfortable. It's hot as hell in here!" He took a deep breath. "I know how you grew up, Tess. I respect your independence. I'm just trying to do the right thing here. If I can't, I can't stick around."

She'd dated her share of losers—artists, bartenders, even a couple of suits—and none of them, not a single one, looked in her cupboards, let alone gave a rat's ass about honor. Doing the right thing. But the problem wasn't that taking the money felt wrong. It was how right it felt, how easily she could add to his burden by letting him shoulder some of hers. Serving his country was the ultimate honor, but no one got rich doing it.

"You don't have all that much more money than I do," she protested, cravenly sidestepping the far more important issue he'd laid at her feet.

For a moment his normal laid-back sense of humor surfaced. "Damn, you're hard on a guy's ego," he said, but just as quickly the smile disappeared into the firm line of his full lips. He shrugged. "I have enough to fix the air conditioner. You don't. I'd give it to you with no strings attached because I love you, but you won't take it."

Shock once again flooded her veins. He pushed away from the wall and a fear more potent than the icy torrent that had immobilized her when he'd stalked out of the shadows settled in the pit of her stomach. "Drew, wait!" she said, and grabbed his arm.

Her grip was strong from lifting kegs and welding heavy, awkward pieces of metal, but he stopped because he wanted to stop. He stopped because she asked.

"You love me?" God, could she sound any more doubtful? Prickly?

"Yeah, Tess. I love you." Soft, even words. She marveled at the strength it took to casually put himself in harm's way, both on duty and off. Right now the soft underbelly of his soul was totally exposed to her, easy to lay open with a few brittle, indifferent words. Until Drew, she'd defined strength by the thickness of walls she built around her heart, the barbed wire fences draping her personality. Compared to his willingness to walk into physical and emotional danger, she was weak. A coward, even.

"You…" She stopped, slid her hand down to clasp his, thinking through how best to handle the hidden sharp edges of another person's feelings. "You've never said that before. Why say it now?"

After a moment, a very long moment, he returned her grip with a gentle squeeze. "I'm a play-the-odds kind of guy, Tess. Odds weren't good I'd hear the words back. Tonight I needed to say it. You don't have to love me back, not right now, but if you can't let me in even a little bit, I can't stay."

The words could have sounded like an ultimatum, an effort to control her through an all-or-nothing choice, but he sounded taut, tightly wound, pushed to the point of no return. She wondered where he'd been, and what he'd seen or done that made him lay it all on the line. Not ready to walk away, but prepared to do so if she kept her defenses up.

Her choice. She swallowed against the ache in her throat, looked at their linked hands, then down farther to their feet, his braced wide, hers snugged together, the right foot curled over the left.

"I don't know how to do this," she said to the chipped, bright blue nail polish on her toes. Hard to admit, but true.

"You don't have to do anything, Tess. I just want to take care of you. Fix your air conditioner. Make sure you stay safe when I'm gone. It won't suck, I promise." He said the words with a crooked smile, tipping her chin up so she met his eyes as he spoke.

"Why?" It was unfathomable to her. In foster care from the time she was eleven, on her own from the day she turned eighteen and the state no longer provided money to cover her food or clothes, she'd long since accepted that if she wanted something—a house no one could make her leave, a degree in industrial art, a client base—she had to scrap for it by herself. "Nobody's wanted to take care of me my whole life. Why would you?"

"Because you're you."

Unable to help herself, she laughed, the sound mocking, derisive. "Yeah, right."

He shrugged, the pain back in his eyes. "This is where the trust part comes in. What's it going to be, Tess?"

Dammit, she'd rather handle rusty scrap metal without gloves than do this, but for the very first time in her life, someone wanted her company on a permanent basis, and not because the state paid for her upkeep. All he wanted her to do was put herself into his hands, into his care.

Terrifying.

Even more terrifying was the thought of holding back, and losing him.

Tension thickened and heated the air around them. Little dots danced at the edges of her vision and she realized she was holding her breath. After a shaky exhalation she took a deep breath, and the scent of him—clean sweat and musk over the harsh tang of no-frills soap—swept through her nostrils, triggering the memory of his unique taste, the silky smooth skin under his wrists, stretched over his hip bones, the underside of his cock. The tension in her muscles eased from her body again. She didn't know how to do this, but Drew had good hands and limitless patience. He'd catch her if she fell.

"Okay," she said, with a nod and a small, tremulous smile.

Fierce exultation gleamed in his eyes. He bent his head and brushed his lips over hers, a sultry kiss that started as the merest pressure, just the tantalizing possibility of something more. Then his tongue lazily traced her lower lip and she opened to him, her breath coming faster, mingling with his. She shifted restlessly as the promise in his mouth trickled down her jaw, hardened her nipples and settled between her thighs.

Then he pulled back. Tess waited a few racing heartbeats, then opened her eyes to find hot, possessive emotion surging in his. In his smooth, easy way he slid his hand into the hair at the nape of her neck. "Okay, what?"

"Okay, I'll take the money to get the air conditioner fixed," she said.

He began a gentle massage, right at the spot where her neck met her skull, the spot where she held all her stress after hours bent over a sketchpad or a project. A thrill shot down her spine even as her shoulders slackened with pleasure.

"And?"

"Hmmm?" That was all she could get out, given his magic touch on her nape.

Her eyes widened at his pointed glance over his shoulder to the open window. At the same time his other hand slid down her arm to encircle her wrist, where he rubbed his thumb over the quickening thump of her pulse. She felt the throb of blood now leaping against his gentle, unyielding pressure. The dark, hot, implacable look in his eyes dropped her gaze to her wrist captured in the cuff of his fingers.

"I'm sorry I slept with the windows open." She was proud of her steady voice, even as her heart thudded hard against her breastbone and fresh sweat broke out under her arms and at the small of her back. *Please let him have forgotten, please, please let him have forgotten...*

"What did I say I'd do if I caught you doing exactly that?"

He hadn't forgotten.

Suddenly his hands on her body felt less like sensual preparation and more like a devious softening up for an interrogation. She didn't need to look into his eyes to note the preternatural energy humming under his skin.

"Drew. No."

"What did I say, Tess? Do you remember the conversation?" The words were liquid, so soft, which was a little scary. Despite the drawl, the sense of humor and the unflinching Southern honor, Drew was anything but soft.

She stayed stubbornly silent through ten pounding heartbeats, twenty, because if she kept quiet, his promise didn't exist. Thirty more beats passed with her gaze focused resolutely on the place where her pulse pounded against the circle of his fingers. Finally, she surrendered.

"We'd been in bed all day and we'd soaked the sheets even though the AC was on. You said it was on its last legs. I said I didn't care because I'd just sleep with the windows open. I'd done it before, and I'd do it again." Unwilling to show fear, she dragged her gaze up to meet his. "And then you said…if I did…you'd spank me until I couldn't sit for a week."

With his back to the windows, stark shadows lay across the planes and angles of his face, concealing most of his expression. His eyes, however, were such a pale blue she could see emotion flickering through them, too fast for her to decipher. His bent head and wide shoulders offered her no protection from the moonlight, but she didn't look away as her heart hammered in her chest and her stomach alternated between circus flip-flops and plummeting to the bottom of her abdomen. And yet at the same time her nipples swelled against the soft material of her tank top and a traitorous heat throbbed in her womb.

In a voice as thick and dark as the still air coalescing into moisture on her skin, he said, "Good thing you don't have a desk job."

Not funny.

She stepped back, twisting her head and arm to pull free, but came up short with her back to the wall. "Drew, you can't possibly mean it. It's…archaic! It's crazy!"

He moved closer, boxing her in. "I meant it, Tess. You knew I meant it when I said it."

Her jaw dropped. A minute ago he was a rational twenty-first century male whose mother had earned her law degree studying nights and weekends, and whose sisters juggled work and kids. That man had disappeared, leaving behind a Drew she recognized only at some level so primitive she hadn't been aware it existed.

"You need this—"

She gasped, somewhere between astonished and outraged. "I do *not*!"

His gentle smile almost hid the intractable look in his eye. "Yes, you do, Tess."

CHAPTER TWO

For the third time in thirty minutes shock ran, electric and searing, through her veins. Suddenly she was as motionless as he was, with no heartbeat, no breathing as she searched his eyes, pale blue and unreadable in the dim light. The hand that had rested lightly on her nape now cupped her cheek, while his thumb brushed her full lips. Then his roughened fingertips trailed along her neck, into the hollow where her collarbones met, then slid down her breastbone before detouring along the lower edge of her ribs and finally dropping to the swell of her hip. He wound his thumb in the string stretched taut there, pulled the thin strip away from her body and slid his fingers into the back of her panties to curve around her bottom.

"You're trembling."

"You're scaring me. Again." She might have sounded believable if her voice had quavered rather than snapped.

"I'm not scaring you. I'm making you mad," he said, calling her bluff without a hint of remorse. "You know nothing bad's gonna happen here. I, on the other hand, came up the street and saw the windows open and half the neighborhood's Latin Kings drinking and hanging around in Mrs. Delgado's driveway."

An impromptu party she hadn't heard over the music. She turned her head to the side, away from the look in his eyes. "I said I was sorry."

"Apology accepted, Tess, but you still get the spanking." His hand tightened on her hip, the pressure constant until she opened her eyes again. He looked back at her, his gaze part wry amusement, part serious intent. "Sometimes pain can feel really, really good."

A dozen smart-mouthed comebacks trembled on the tip of her tongue, but in the end the agitation roiling inside her kept her from voicing a single one. She shoved at his shoulder and ducked under his arm, hurrying down the stairs and across the peeling linoleum to the kitchen sink. She opened the faucet as far as it would go. Cold water streamed into the scratched aluminum bowl. She scooped handfuls of water to her mouth, then splashed her face.

He'd lost his mind. That was the only explanation. He was completely insane if he thought she'd let him spank her. Yes, she'd left the windows open, but that was no reason for him to make good on a lazy promise made at the tail end of four hours of sex. Truth be told, they were nowhere near vanilla in bed, but let a Navy SEAL spank her, for God's sake? He was certifiable!

Except he sounded sane, assured and totally in control.

Expecting him hard on her heels, she shut off the water and turned, but the stairs were empty, the creaky floorboards above her silent. Would he forget about it? He looked haggard with exhaustion, dark smudges under his eyes visible even in the dim light of her room. Maybe if she gave him enough time he'd fall asleep and they could laugh this off in the morning. Or maybe he'd storm down the stairs, drag her to the sofa and blister her butt. Moments passed, then stretched into a minute without sound or movement.

Fine. He could sit up there until he roasted.

Her mind replayed his words…*put yourself in my place…not as badly as you scared me…half the neighborhood's Latin Kings drinking and hanging around in Mrs. Delgado's driveway…not as badly as you scared me…*

Well, that was an accomplishment to put on her résumé. She'd managed to scare a SEAL, an individual trained to handle any circumstance at any time with whatever meager tools and resources he had at hand. She'd scared him.

But she'd known when she wedged opened the windows with a small shim that she wasn't just dealing with her poverty line life. She was defying the only rule he'd felt strongly enough to voice. Despite his current incarnation as a dominant alpha male, Drew was laid-back, relaxed, beyond tolerant of her unusual hours, jobs, hair color and friends. Besides the windows, he simply let her be. Of course, a highly trained professional special operative in the United States Navy should have more on his mind than fussing over her rainbow hair and shabby wardrobe.

Okay, she got it. This had to be about his job, which called for extended, unbroken focus, and if he was worried about her, he might falter at a very deadly task. Given the life-or-death scenarios he faced, the last thing she wanted to do was distract him. She'd let him down, wronged him by disobeying a very specific request. If he felt that strongly about this, then fine. He wouldn't hurt her. She knew that.

Best to get it over with.

She turned and climbed the stairs with far more reluctance than she'd shown on her way down. Drew sat on the bed in her room, his eyes closed, his back to the wall, one leg stretched out in front of him, the other pulled up. His arm rested on his bent knee, the hand dangling forward while the other hand lay on his thigh. A wide swath of moonlight illuminated his face and body, and she saw the tendons of his hands running under skin dusted with fine, white-blond hair. Three knuckles were bruised, nothing unusual.

His hands had fascinated her from their first meeting—on a brilliantly sunny, San Diego, late winter day after a storm, when the surf pounded the beach in waves the length and height of tractor-trailers and the sand was damp from rain. Drawn to the crash of the surf and the clouds scudding across the sky, she'd spent the entire day sculpting an enormous, whimsical castle complete with thick walls, a moat, drawbridges, and turrets with gargoyles, perched atop a mound of sand carved into unassailable cliffs. Late in the afternoon several surfers who'd survived despite their death wish stopped to examine her work.

Drew was one of them. A couple inches

under six feet, he was so leanly muscled that in his unzipped wet suit she could see veins, tendons, ligaments running under his skin. It was his hands she'd watched, however, as he and his friends circled the castle, sizing up the fanciful structure before identifying weak points and strategizing an attack. Nicks, scabs and scars covered his long, tapering fingers and the backs of his hands, while his palms and fingertips bore calluses from physical use. His hands skimmed over the packed sand, almost but not quite touching the painstakingly molded shapes as he argued with a buddy about climbing techniques. Muscles roped around his wrists and forearms, and his biceps, triceps, deltoid, trapezius and abdominal muscles flexed and released under his skin.

Any San Diego-raised girl knew navy when she saw it. Marriage-minded girls could pick out officers blocks away. After three years of bartending near the base, Tess correctly guessed rank with nine out of ten guys, and knew the SEALs from the wannabes. Drew was the real deal, and guys like him, with their pick of the beach bunnies, normally didn't give her the time of day. But he'd looked at her, then at the castle, then back at her again.

***

"You did this?"

She surveyed seven hours of work that would wash away with the next rain, and shrugged. "Yes."

"Nobody helped you?"

"No."

He took in her rolled up jeans with the muddy knees, her bare, dirty feet with bright purple toenails matching the purple streaks in her blonde-for-now hair, windblown from two braids, her shapeless hoodie sweater. His eyes showed a frank interest her petite, semi-Goth self rarely attracted.

"Impressive."

After a murmured conversation he transferred his board to a buddy. She stood silently next to him and watched his friends load up their trucks and leave.

She smiled at him, ready to play the game that would put him in his place at arm's length. "How are you going to get back to the base?"

He squinted into the setting sun, then at the nearly empty parking lot, then finally at her. A quirky grin crossed his face. "I was hoping if I bought you dinner you'd give me a ride."

"I'd think about it, except I don't have a car."

This time she spoke without a hint of emotion,

as if his unexpected invitation hadn't sent a secret thrill through her. In return she expected disbelief, irritation, even a bit of blame for being so pathetic as to ride the bus. Instead, he threw back his head and laughed at himself, at her, at life, it didn't matter, because she was done. With his self-deprecating sense of humor and deft, confident hands, he'd won this round.

While she stood beside him and tried not to gawk at his hands or the gorgeous, anatomy-textbook planes of his torso, he pulled a cell phone out of his backpack and sent a quick text message. Then he introduced himself, helped her rinse her tools and pack them in the canvas tote that held the trash from her picnic lunch. Almost right away a black truck and a red sports car pulled into the nearly empty parking lot. Silent and efficient, a bulky bald guy got out of the truck, tossed a set of keys to Drew and slid into the passenger seat of the sports car. With a spray of gravel and mud the red vehicle zoomed back onto the highway.

He palmed the keys and looked at her. "Mexican? Thai? Italian? Your choice."

Game over.

"Well?"

The brusque question called her back from the windy day by the ocean to the stifling confines of her bedroom, and the black-clad man waiting silently on her bed.

She spoke in an even, measured tone of voice intended to hide the exasperation simmering inside her. "I get it. You asked me not to do something. I did it, anyway. That was disrespectful. If we're going to be together I can't be a burden while you're…working. In the future I'll do whatever it takes to stay as safe as possible. And if you need to…spank me…to work this out, I'm ready."

There. An admission of guilt plus the proper recognition for his demanding career. That ought to do it.

After another snort of disbelief, he opened his eyes and turned his head, fixing her with an uncompromising look. "You think I'm doing this for me? Wrong, Tess. Your apology was sincere. I trust you won't do this again. The spanking is for you."

Exasperation exploded into slitty-eyed irritation. "I cannot believe you think I need—"

His lifted hand cut off her words, then he turned his wrist and beckoned her forward. "You said you were ready. Come here."

***

The temper that got her screamed at, or worse, in every foster home she'd lived in surged red-hot in her throat, but she drew breath, closed her eyes and let it out as she counted to ten. He had a point. She didn't *get* his point, but dominating or hurting her wasn't the issue. She knew that. "Fine, fine. Let's just get this over with," she muttered under her breath as she stepped through the doorway and stalked toward the bed.

A hint of a smile danced around the corners of his mouth before the beckoning hand switched to the closed fist meaning *halt*. "Take off your top."

The heat in his eyes and his intractable tone flipped a switch in her brain. All the confused protests tumbling around in her rational mind sputtered in a crackle of static, then shut off, but her body reacted automatically. She tugged the wet, clinging fabric over her head and let the shirt drop to the floor as she bent forward.

While she'd intended nothing more than using her hair to hide the aroused flush flooding her cheekbones, a hitch in Drew's even breathing as he beckoned to her again told her he wasn't immune to her downcast eyes and nearly naked body. Her hair fell dark against the upper swells of her breasts, and her white panties stood out even against her pale skin. As politically incorrect as it was, she couldn't blame her thudding heart and watery knees on nerves alone. The stark reality was she was all but naked as she crawled up onto the bed to accept his punishment for her disobedience, and her female, animal body seemed to be operating on an entirely different frequency from her rational brain. Sheer erotic arousal pumped through her veins.

Drew lifted his hands out of the way so she could lie facedown across his lap in a strange, awkward and more than a little embarrassing alignment of their bodies.

"Move forward," he said, his voice soft yet firm.

In response to his command she shimmied forward, centering her bottom directly over his thighs. His discarded black watchman's cap lay a few inches away. She gathered it to her and rested her face on her folded forearms as images of how this looked flashed against the movie screen of her mind. Mostly naked, over his lap, her bottom perfectly situated for swats.

"Pull down your panties."

Red, telling heat bloomed in her cheeks at the thought of reaching back and baring her bottom for him. The pendulum of her emotions swung wildly between a rather disturbing excitement and sheer vexation. She clenched her teeth to bite back a furious response, then turned her face away from him and reached back to hook her thumbs in the elastic edge of the string bikini briefs. With a little squirming and some help from him, she got her panties down, lifting just enough to let him tug the soaked panel from between her legs. She expected him to slide them down and off, but he left the white fabric at midthigh.

He stroked his palm over the curve of first one cheek, then the other, the touch soft, gentle, so seductive she let out her breath in a trembling rush, and with the exhalation, melted into his powerful thighs. A lush blend of arousal, embarrassment and nerves made her wiggle her hips in a figure-eight on his lap. When she made contact with his erection, hard and ready against his fly, his hand tightened briefly on her ass.

"Let's try again. Why did you leave the windows open?"

Fuck counting to ten. For that matter, fuck *him*! Hot, aroused, sweating, confused and emotionally reeling, she sucked in air and pushed up onto her hands and knees. "Damn it, Drew!" she all but shouted as she turned to look at him. "You know why!"

The muscles in his arm flexed as the hand at the small of her back forced her flat, then *crack!* A resounding smack landed on the left side of her bottom. Tess jumped and yelped as fire spread from the point of impact.

"Wrong answer."

"Drew, you can't—"

Crack! She yelped again, a shock wave of pain blistering through her ass.

"Whatever you think I can't do, I can. The windows, Tess. Why?"

If he intended to keep this up until he got the answer he wanted, she could see the benefit of coming around to his point of view. The only problem was she didn't know what he wanted her to say, and she told him that.

Crack! "Think about it, Tess," he said, with a low, peremptory chuckle. "Take as long as you need."

He was *amused*? "You…you…*jerk*!"

The crack of flesh against flesh ricocheted around her bedroom. She jumped again, felt his hand spread in warning against her lower back, and muffled her startled cry in her folded arms.

It *hurt*.

Another measured smack landed in the same place, flat on her bottom. Raw sensation expanded in pulsar waves as he moved to the other cheek and administered five smacks there. A hot ache swelled and spread, much as pleasure did during long, lazy afternoons in bed. He switched sides again, settling into a methodical pace, not so hard and rapid that she felt battered in either body or soul, yet not slow and light enough for her to surface from the pain of each smack's sharp impact.

He worked at his task while she twitched and wriggled with each stroke, gripping his cap and trying to choke back the gasps fluttering from her throat. The weight of his hand near her center of gravity anchored her, body and soul. The strength of his thighs under her stomach and legs, the solidity of his abdomen at her side all kept her focused on the painful, erotically charged, emotionally laden moment.

What the *hell* was this all about if it wasn't about her dogged independence and how that affected him? She wouldn't do it again. He trusted her to keep her word, and he was certainly keeping his. He'd said he would spank her, and here she was, naked and facedown on her quilt, while his relentless hand moved from

cheek to cheek and he steadfastly ignored her stifled yelps, which threatened to become sobs as
the stinging grew to burning. Despite the unde-
niable sexy undertone, she knew this wasn't his
first choice of activities on his first night home.
He could have ignored the windows, the broken
air conditioner and her crushing financial strain
in favor of simple sex, pizza delivery and sleep.
He could have yelled at her and left. Worse, he
could have just turned around in the street.

But here he was. Doing what he'd said he'd do.

He hadn't left when he found the evidence of
her disobedience. He'd stayed, and as painful as
it was, he'd kept his word. He'd stayed.

He would stay. No matter what she did.

The smacks continued inexorably, but realization broke through the burgeoning ache. Deep
down, she'd doubted his commitment. She
thought he would disappear for real, not because
he was mobilized. He'd just leave one day and
not come back. Like her father, and then her
mother. If she goaded him into it, then she could
control when it happened.

That's why she'd needed the spanking, both
for her lack of trust, and as physical proof that he
would keep his word. She could trust him to give
her what he said he would. What she needed.

"I get it," she gasped over the rhythmic slaps. "I get it! Drew, please!"

His hand came to rest again on her now stinging, heated bottom, leaving an expectant, vibrant silence. Slowly, carefully, she relaxed her taut, quivering muscles, subsiding into his lap, but while the muscle tension eased, liquid flame burned in her swollen, wet folds. He reached out and gathered her hair in his hand, sending it spilling over her shoulder. Surprised by the temperate touch, she turned her face and looked back at him.

"Why did you leave the windows open?" he asked gently.

The truth hurt. It really, really did. More than her ass, in fact. "Because I wanted to see what you'd do if I did."

"Even though I told you what I'd do." He wasn't asking. He knew. He'd known before she even walked into her bedroom.

There was a time and place for obstinate defiance. This wasn't it. "Yes."

"And what did you learn, Tess?" His voice was so soft and open she could hardly believe it came from the same man who'd purposefully paddled her into next week.

"To trust you." She took a deep breath and let

it rush out onto the thin quilt under her hot cheek. "I learned you always keep your word."

"Always." The single word hummed with the unshakable confidence of a United States Navy SEAL. "You tell me to go and I'm gone. But you can't make me abandon you because you act up." He caressed her stinging butt. "You can earn yourself another spanking, no problem. But I'm here for the duration."

She let out another shuddering sigh as his words sank deep into her psyche, absolution and commitment rushing in to replace fear and abandonment. But her body still had a pressing need for relief. Undulating on his lap generated a sharp, longing twinge when her pubic bone made contact with his hard thigh. She'd never felt this way before, never had urgent, immediate desire thumping under her skin while she lay limp and pliable against his hard body. Soft give and sharp need melting together, and oh, how she wanted him to assuage the ache between her thighs.

Possessive admiration softened the line of his jaw as Drew slowly scanned her from toes to calves to thighs, lingering at her ass before sliding his gaze up the length of her spine, to her brown hair draped around her sweaty shoulders, then to her face. She didn't turn away, but let the heat throbbing in her bottom reflect in her eyes as she lifted her butt against his hand.

Admiration gave way to molten lust. "You want me to finish this," he said, but he wasn't asking.

All she could do was nod.

He raised his hand and she closed her eyes again, but this time she lifted into the stroke that fell not on the marked, throbbing skin, but rather on the soft inner curve where her buttocks met her thighs. The blow, lighter than the others but carefully placed, sent a sharp shard of heat flashing into her pussy. Once again she jumped and gasped, but even to her own ears the gasp wasn't one of pain, or shock, but the sound she made when he flicked his tongue against her clit. Which was exactly how this felt, except from the inside out. It felt as if he'd struck sparks in her clit, and the tender flesh swelled in demand.

She peered over her shoulder again. His eyes locked with hers and he deliberately raised his hand, landing another smack in the same place, but on the opposite cheek. Sharp, swift pleasure speared through her. The slap was different, the landing spot different, the sensations different, the moan different. Deeper. Throatier. Could have been lust, could have been pain.

He paused. "Too much?"

Yes, but oh, so good. "Don't stop," she groaned, winding her fingers through the hair gathered at the nape of her neck before she buried her face in her arm again.

His cock pulsed hard against her hip bone before his hand fell. The pace was slower, giving the pleasure time to build through the fire that exploded with each crack of his hand against her bottom. She found herself rocking back into each stroke, waiting for each one to fall, focusing on the ache expanding in her throbbing clit. The soles of her feet burned, and her nipples rubbed against the worn cotton quilt as she gasped and writhed under each blow.

Finally, when the ache threatened to destroy her, when she teetered on the edge of all-consuming pleasure, a smack landed that detonated the burgeoning heat. Orgasm flashed bright inside her and rolled to the tips of her fingers and toes as she threw her head back and let out a soft, high-pitched moan.

When she could rouse herself she felt his hands stroking her back, bottom and thighs. Little tingles chased through the steady pulsations in her ass. She let her arms fall beside her face, gathered her strength and pushed back. As she moved, he pulled her panties off, then put his hands under her elbows to help her upright, supporting her but letting her situate herself as she pleased.

What pleased her was to straddle his lap, *carefully* ease her bottom back against his thighs, and look him right in the eye while she tucked her hair behind her ears, wiped at her own eyes with the heels of her hands, licked her swollen lips. He watched each movement, then cupped her cheek and brushed his thumb over her mouth. He threaded his hand through her hair and pulled her down for a hot, swift kiss, his tongue flickering over her lips until she softened against him.

His gaze searched hers; his fingers gently rubbed her scalp. She returned the look, hiding nothing, avoiding nothing. What he saw must have pleased him because his lips quirked into a grin.

"You okay?"

Good question. Her heart pounded, whether from the exertion in the hot, muggy, still air, or from the pitch and heave of her emotions in the last hour, she couldn't say. The rough material of his damp BDUs chafed her tender skin. A new tenderness drifted inside her, unfamiliar yet not the slightest bit scary.

"My ass hurts," she said bluntly, "but yeah, I'm okay. Tomorrow I'll make an appointment to get the air conditioner fixed. And…um…thank you. For loaning me—"

"Giving me, " he corrected.

"Giving me the money."

"My pleasure," he said, but the wicked gleam in his eye betrayed the formal tone and words.

She trailed her fingers across his beautiful cheekbones and lips, down over the glittering gold scruff on his chin to dab at the sweat pooling in the hollow of his throat, then down his abdomen to snag her fingers in his waistband and press her pussy against the hard ridge in his pants. His shirt was so sodden she could probably wring it out like a wet rag. The gleam in his eyes went from wicked to intent.

"You liked that," she said, but the accusation was a mild one. There was a thin line between play and punishment.

He wasn't a liar, so he just gave her a wink.

"How red is my ass?"

"A pretty rosy pink," he said huskily, as he throbbed hard against her soft folds.

Interesting. "You going to spank me again?"

Heat flared in his eyes and he tightened his grip on her hips. "If you need it, or if you ask me very, very nicely."

"That sounds promising," she started, as she leaned forward and set her hands on his ribs. The quick, indrawn breath he gave at the pressure of her hands on his chest made her stop, then sit back. He loosened his grasp, but his lips pulled tight over clenched teeth. A couple seconds later his breath eased out and his jaw relaxed.

Oh God, oh God... "Drew?" she asked, and began to tug his sweat-saturated T-shirt from his pants.

"Easy, Tess," he said, but his voice was resigned as he submitted to her efforts to undress him, sitting forward and lifting his arms over his head so she could pull his shirt off and toss it to the floor with a wet thud.

Once again, icy fear wicked through her veins. The left side of his torso was a mass of bruises, some faded to yellowish-green, others the fresh deep purple of recent blows. A gash too deep to be a scratch but not deep enough to need stitches bisected his torso from just under his right pectoral down to his left hip bone. Much deeper and he would have been gutted.

"Drew," she breathed, her fingers trailing over

the abused skin. "What happened? Did some-body *hit* you?"

The words sounded astonishingly stupid as they left her mouth, but he just gave a little smile at the incredulous tone of her voice. "A little dust-up. Ain't no big thing, baby," he said, mock-ing mortal danger in the Alabama drawl that lingered despite nine years in California.

Which meant he couldn't talk about it. He'd matter-of-factly explained that anything really serious would mean members of his team at her front door and an introductory meeting with his family next to a flag-draped casket.

"Are your ribs broken?"

"Not even cracked," he said.

She looked back at the vicious, spreading bruises and quirked an eyebrow at him, but let it slide. There was no point in pestering him for details he couldn't provide. If someone got close enough to do this kind of intimate damage, what-ever he'd done hadn't been the usual clockwork "in and out without a shot fired" mission. With her hand at his nape she kissed his forehead, then rested hers against his.

"I love you, Tess," he said, his voice husky. "It's good to be home."

He needed a shower, a meal, twelve hours of

sleep and about half a tube of antibacterial ointment, but fussing and hand-wringing went over as well as sleeping with the windows open. She pushed her concern aside, sat up and affected a disbelieving pout. "Really? Because from my perspective, you being home means me scared witless and spanked. But I'm glad it was good for you."

One golden eyebrow quirked up at her sassing. "That wasn't good for you? Because it sounded damned good at the end there."

"Okay, it was pretty good," she said with a mock eye roll.

"Pretty good? I can do better," he promised, then those seductive, dangerous hands went to the fly of his cargo pants and began to slip buttons from holes to free his straining shaft. His knuckles brushed against her damp mound, coming closer with each undone button. He pushed himself off the bed with both hands, lifting his hips for Tess to tug the clinging, sweaty fabric down. The pants made a louder, squishier thud than his shirt had when she flung them heedlessly behind her. From her crouched position she kissed her way up his long, leanly muscled legs. After a brief, assessing look at his cock, straining thick and dark red from the blond nest of curls, she ran her tongue up the underside, the taste and scent of sex and sweat a heady aphrodisiac.

She kissed each hip bone, then licked the ridges of muscle forming his abdomen. Each wicked bruise received a gentle touch of her lips, as did the edges of the slice through his skin. She poured words not yet spoken into the caress of her breath, the flutter of her tongue against his skin, the not-quite-gentle pressure of her teeth against each nipple in turn. His breathing had slowed and softened with her ministrations, but stopped altogether at the sharp pressure, before easing out in a guttural groan.

She peeked down to see his cock pulse away from his abdomen as a pearly bead formed at the tip. "Wow," she said as she straddled him again. "You did miss me."

"I always do," he said, cupping her ass to pull her snug against his erection.

She affected a wince as his big hands flexed against her tender bottom. "Think twice before you work over your favorite playground," she said, the admonishment negated by her breathy voice…and the explosive orgasm.

Laughter gleamed in his eyes as he obediently slid his hands up her rib cage to her breasts, teasing her nipples as he massaged the soft flesh. "I like to play here, too."

"Ummm...yes," she whispered as he pinched and rolled the tender buds. Electric sensation flashed from her nipples to her clit. She bent forward, this time resting her hands on his shoulders, grinding a little as she kissed him. His tongue flicked against her parted lips, and with a soft moan she opened to him. Heat flashed between them as she rubbed her tongue against his, letting out a little sob as he nipped at her lower lip, then slid one hand into her hair to hold her for his mouth.

"Drew, please," she moaned. "I want to come with you inside me."

God, did she want that. She didn't idealize a relationship with any active-duty naval officer, let alone a SEAL. *Relationship* meant deployments, mobilizations, missions. It meant unexplained absences and weeks of worry. It meant seeing bruises, scrapes and scars on his body, pain and blankness in his eyes. It meant nightmares.

But with Drew *relationship* meant a love as strong and fierce as the commitment he made to his country, and his team. It meant a soft place to land. It meant living with a wild, focused intensity when he was home, starting here in their bed. For now, empty solo orgasms were a thing of the past. She wanted to drop into the abyss with him as deep in her body as he was in her heart.

He unfisted his hand from her hair and set it on her hip as she reached for the condoms in the nightstand, then scooted back a bit to tear one open. Their fingers tangled as they rolled it down his shaft, but after that it was all her. She braced one hand on his shoulder and used the other to pull his erection away from his ridged abdomen. His breathing harshened, quickened as he looked down and watched her center her wet, open body over his tip and slowly engulf him.

His eyelids dropped as she slid down. "Fuck yeah," he growled as she began to move. His head fell back, coming to rest against the white plaster wall behind her bed. "Oh, fuck, Tess. So good."

The first fast, furious time had taken the edge off, but only the second session, with its prolonged, intimate connection, smoothed all the emotional edges roughened by his absence. She kept her tempo fluid and relentless, building the pleasure for him in thin, fine layers, much as she would use heat and compounds to add a patina to metalwork. His throat worked as his eyes slid shut and his lips parted, his breath easing out in one long, soft exhalation. She flicked her tongue against his lower lip as she tweaked his nipples, and he inhaled and arched, thudding into her with enough force to make her squeak.

"So how nicely do I have to ask to get another spanking?"

His head snapped forward at the question, a hot, tortured gleam in his eyes. "Very nicely," he said, low and rough.

She spread her legs and ground against him on the next downstroke, burying him to the hilt in her hot, wet passage. "I'm not asking now, you understand," she whispered. "Just getting an idea for next time. You want me on my knees when I ask?"

He fisted his hands in her loose, damp hair before his head dropped back against the wall again, exposing the pulse pounding in the base of his throat. His cock throbbed inside her. "Jesus, Tess."

"I'll take that as a yes," she said, then pressed her lips to his jaw. "Let's see…me on my knees…naked…my mouth wet from sucking your cock…would that be nice enough for you? I'd say please."

"Ask like that and I'll give you anything you want," he said as he shifted, surging forward and pulling her head back, to suck not quite gently at the skin over her collarbone.

She rode his movements, arching into him, skin slick and slippery as she rubbed against his torso. Her orgasm swelled, gathering strength with each gliding, increasingly heated move. "You going to spank me for teasing you?"

That was the final straw. Strong and sure, he rolled her to her back, then pulled out, spreading her legs wide with his hard thighs and pressing her hands into the bed beside her head. "I'm going to fuck you for teasing me," he growled. "Eventually."

He braced himself above her, their only points of contact his hair-roughened thighs against her sore bottom, and his fingers, interlocked with hers. Hard kisses dropped onto her plump lips, stifling her fretful moans, as sweat dropped from his collarbone and temples. When she quieted, he held himself above her with taut control, surveying her wet, pert breasts. He bent his head and blew gently on one nipple, watched it tighten, then treated the other to the same torture.

"They're almost as pink as your ass," he said.

She shuddered at the image. When his teeth closed on an erect nipple she let out a whimper, but the insistent pressure and his flickering licks against the trapped bud quickly made her moan. The rough stubble on his cheeks rasped against her soft skin as he worked, moving from one nipple to the other until both were raspberry-red.

"Perfect," he said, as she desperately yanked against his tight grip, trying to free their locked fingers.

He left her nipples throbbing in the heated night air, and licked his way down her breastbone to her navel, moving their joined hands as he shifted between her legs. Their interlaced fingers ended up under her sore ass, and she trembled at the submissive sensuality of using her hands to lift her wet, aching pussy to his mouth. The breadth of his shoulders spread her legs wide for the lash of his tongue. He flicked, he licked, he nibbled, all in his own time, driving her up the ladder of desire until she arched and fell away into blackness.

The luscious, slick stroke of his cock into her satiated body brought her back into the moonlit room. Poised above her, sheer possessive agony etched into his face, he plunged into her, his elbow braced at her shoulder to keep her from sliding away on the sweat-dampened sheets, his hand gripping her bottom without mercy, his hips spreading her open to his pounding body. Mindful of his bruised ribs, she gripped the small of his back, then wrapped her heels around his calves and arched to meet him.

When her orgasm came there was no falling this time, only annihilation. She exploded, sinking her teeth into his shoulder as she flew apart. With one last, tremendous thrust he buried himself to the hilt inside her. He shuddered, sweat dripping from his jaw to plunk on her collarbone, then he buried his head in the curve of her neck, his shoulders heaving. Long minutes passed while she simply stroked the damp skin of his back, breathing slowly to encourage the subtle loosening of his muscles, his heart rate returning to its normal slow thud against his breastbone.

Eventually he rolled off her and staggered into the bathroom, giving a muffled curse when he banged his shoulder on the door frame. She giggled and flopped onto her stomach. He came back and eased himself down next to her, on his back. His uninjured side was closest, so she cuddled into him and felt his arm come around her.

"Damn, Tess. You pack a powerhouse punch for a hundred pounds and change."

"It's not me. Those ribs are cracked and you probably haven't slept more than an hour a day for the last four weeks." She kissed him, soft and slow and sweet, then gave in to curiosity. "Where are your boots?"

"Locked in the trunk of my car with my duffel. I'll get 'em in a minute," he said. "You working tomorrow?"

"In my studio, but I switched shifts at The Blue Dog. The developer called while you were gone. He really liked the balcony I did for that house in Balboa Park. He wants to see staircase designs by Monday."

Drew lifted his head to look at her, a delighted grin splitting his face. "Tess, that's fantastic." His head dropped back and sweat trickled down his temple. "Fuck, it's hot in here. Let's grab a quick shower and go celebrate. Somewhere air-conditioned."

He slid his legs over the edge of the bed and sat up with a wince. Before he could get to his feet she went to her knees, slipped her arms around his neck and whispered into his ear the words she'd doodled in swirling calligraphy with the sketches of staircases and his face. "I love you, too, Drew."

Despite injuries, exhaustion and exertion, he pulled her around him, into his lap. "Yeah?" he asked, his eyes searching hers.

She gave him a soft smile. "Yeah. Welcome home."

Cuffing Kate

By Alison Tyler

Called a "Trollop with a Laptop" by East Bay Express, a "Literary Siren" by Good Vibrations, and "Erotica's Own Superwoman" by The East Bay Literary Examiner, **Alison Tyler** has made being naughty a full-time job. Her sultry short stories have appeared in more than 100 anthologies including Sex for America edited by Stephen Elliott, Purple Panties edited by Zane, and Best Women's Erotica 2011 edited by Violet Blue. Her stories have appeared in Playgirl Magazine, Penthouse Variations, and Fishnet. She is the editor of more than 50 erotic anthologies, including Alison's Wonderland, Naked Erotica, Naughty Fairy Tales from A to Z, and With This Ring, I Thee Bed. Her 25 novels include Tiffany Twisted, Melt With You, and Something About Workmen. Ms. Tyler is loyal to coffee (black), lipstick (red), and tequila (straight). She has tattoos, but no piercings; a wicked tongue, but a quick smile; and bittersweet memories, but no regrets. She believes the rain won't fall if she doesn't bring an umbrella, prefers hot and dry to cold and wet, and loves to spout her favorite motto: "You can sleep when you're dead." She chooses Led Zeppelin over the Beatles, the Cure over the Smiths, and the Stones over everyone-yet although she appreciates good rock, she has a pitiful weakness for '80s hair bands. In all things important, she remains faithful to her husband of 15 years, but she still can't choose just one perfume.

"I can't fucking believe it!"

A debate is a game. There is always a winner and a loser. This is why I don't debate. Sonia sees things differently. She never loses.

"What's up?"

My roommate slammed into my bedroom so hard that the door hit the wall. Another ding in the plaster. I shoved the dirty book I was reading under my pillow, but Sonia didn't even look my way. She was already pacing. I kept quiet about the fact that she'd entered my room without knocking. Sonia loves to make an entrance, which means that she rarely ever knocks.

"The fucking bastard."

I stared at her, curious. I'd never seen her like this before. Well, that's not entirely true. Sonia's hot-tempered. She gets all riled up during debates about war in the Middle East or why *tofurkey* is the wonder food. But this was different. Her cheeks were flushed a bright fuchsia and her dark espresso-hued eyes looked huge and wild.

"Did you have a fight?" I asked tentatively.

"A fight? No, not a fight." She bit off each word as if chewing on a piece of that nasty papaya fruit leather she buys at the local health food store. I watched her stomp out of my room, heard her clomping toward the kitchen in her vegan no-cows-were-killed boots. Silently I trailed behind her, dumbfounded as she pulled a Guinness from the fridge—one of *my* beers. I'd never seen Sonia drink an alcoholic beverage.

"Then what happened?"

"The bastard. He actually tried to…"

She swallowed a huge gulp of the brew and leaned against our fridge. The Well-behaved Women Rarely Make History magnet was poised over her head on the freezer. It read like a caption. I waited, but she didn't continue.

"Tried to…" I prompted.

"He really thought I would let him…"

"Let him…" I echoed, faux helpfully.

"Never mind. Chalk the experience up to a bad fucking date."

"What did he try to do?" And why did I care so much?

Sonia strode into the living room, threw herself onto our thrift-store sofa and grabbed the ugly comforter her great-aunt had crocheted. She was calming down. I could tell. Maybe she wouldn't tell me the rest. Sometimes she kept things from me. This is why I read her diary on a daily basis.

"He was kinky," she said with finality.

Sonia was decidedly *not* kinky. That's mostly what I'd discovered by reading the tightly cramped handwritten pages in her recycled-paper journal. She wasn't kinky, and she wasn't that into sex, and she wasn't that into men. But she didn't seem to realize this last fact yet. Maybe when she discovered the latter the former would change.

"What do you mean, 'kinky'?"

She shrugged and turned on Bill Maher, dismissing me by not responding. I thought of pushing the issue, of trying to take our roommate status to a higher level. Sonia considered us good friends, but we weren't. She never shared her feelings with me, and she didn't seem to care about my own. Mostly she preached her beliefs in my general direction—trying to guilt me into giving up things that she thought I shouldn't do, or eat, or drink, or think.

I went to my room, consumed by visions of the man she'd been out with. Jules Rodriguez. I knew him from school. Senior. Handsome. Of course, I understood perfectly why he'd asked Sonia on a date. She looked as if she'd be hell-fire in bed. Anyone with an ounce of imagination could envision her in the heat of the moment— long twists of black curls spiraling as she moved, huge eyes glazed with lust. Aside from that, she dressed like sex on wheels: tight clothes in electric colors, earrings that jangled when she walked. Men were drawn to her. She baited them, and then dismissed them. Over and over and over.

I thought again about the recent one. Jules. What naughty thing had he suggested to Sonia? And why did I so desperately want him to try that same thing out on me, whatever the trick might have been?

My mind made an instant laundry list of devi-ant possibilities: *Spanking? Anal? Sex toys?*

For a moment, I considered returning to the living room. Sonia *was* drinking her first beer, after all. Maybe she would have looser lips than usual. But I didn't feel up to listening to a full-on rant. Hopefully she would write about the situa-tion in her diary. Tomorrow when she went to class, I could sneak in and read every filthy little detail.

Except maybe I couldn't wait that long.

Jules lived in an apartment down the hill from campus. I knew because I'd known him before Sonia. We'd shared one class together—a cozy little 500-student Art History class. I also served him his daily caffeine infusion as barista at the central campus coffee bar. From my vantage point, I could spy him often in the quad. I hate to admit that I followed him, so let's just say that one day our paths crossed in town, and I watched as he entered a retro white stucco apartment with wrought-iron railings on the balconies.

Sonia may look like she'd be a good lay—but I thought Jules looked like he knew how to get inside a woman's head. He was tall and lean, given to dressing simply in battered blue jeans and a khaki jacket. In between serving up shots of espresso, I'd drawn pictures of the two of us entwined. My canvas: white paper napkins. To my dismay, he simply hadn't chosen the right woman.

What had he asked her for? What had he wanted to do?

"I'm going out," I told Sonia as I passed behind the sofa to the door.

"Where?"

"A walk."

"If you go by *Juiceeze*, pick me up a smoothie," she said. "Carrot and ginger, please. That beer was foul. You shouldn't drink those."

I didn't answer. I worship Guinness.

"And you don't need any more coffee," she added as I began to shut the door. "Putting caffeine in your body is like depositing counterfeit money in your bank account." These were the pearls of wisdom Sonia tossed out every day. I let them roll under the dresser like dust bunnies on roller skates.

Without a plan, I walked by Jules's apartment. Then I stopped and looked at the shades on the windows. What if I went up and knocked on his door? What if I forced him to tell me exactly what had happened? I could imagine the way he would look at me. Every day, he bought java from the coffee bar, but we'd never actually spoken more than the most casual chitchat. What kind of crazy person confronts a virtual stranger about his sex life?

I took a step. I spun around. I went home.

Patience is one of my only virtues. This strength comes with the fact that I have had to wait for nearly everything I've ever wanted. I'm not complaining. This is my truth. But is this also why I envy Sonia? Men fall into her lap. Instructors trip over themselves to hear what tidbit of wisdom she has to offer. This time, all I had to do was bide my time until she left for class.

Her diary was exactly where she always kept it. Sonia would never think of me as a snoop. She lives so much on the surface, she never stirs her unvarnished toenails in the water to see if there's depth.

I sat on the edge of her bed, my hands shaking as I found the latest entry. Jules had asked her to dinner, but not at a restaurant, at his house. That was smart of him. Sonia has such restrictive eating habits. There are few decent vegan hotspots in the vicinity. He'd poured wine, which she accepted, even if she didn't take a sip. Why had she gone to his place? From all the previous entries I'd read, Sonia had never gone home with a man.

Her own words answered the question for me.

He was a gentleman, and I loved the way he spoke. His words were eloquent as he described the text we're reading.

So what had happened? Sonia bored me for two paragraphs as she described her own feelings about the text then wrote a bit about how Jules had offered to coach her before her next debate. Finally there it was. A word leaped out at me, big and bold and black: Handcuffs.

He said I was beautiful, but out of control. The way I had to gesture when I spoke, pacing, like an animal. He said he wanted to bind me down, so that I couldn't move, and then he would see— we *would see—what I had to say.*

I put the book down. I knew the ending already. She hadn't let him bind her down. But I was aflutter at the thought that this man was so attractive, so intelligent, so kinky, and yet so unable to read the fact that Sonia was not the type of girl he was after.

All year, I'd watched different men discover this fact for a variety of reasons. Sonia was like a coveted chocolate from the center of a scarlet, heart-shaped box—once you bit in, you found you'd made a disappointing choice. Too much nougat. Too many nuts.

I'm the opposite. My co-worker, Dan, described me as WYSIWYG: What you see is what you get. Simple attire: well-worn Levi's and an oxford button-down. Simple hairstyle: long and straight to the middle of my back. No frills, maybe, but simplicity can be sexy, too. Calvin Klein built his empire on clean-cut lines, didn't he? Not that I could compare myself with the models in CK ads, but I have always striven for that sharp elegance. Black and white. No gray.

I reread the part about being bound again. And again. Reluctantly I put her book back, exactly where she kept the journal, and went to my own room to touch myself. This was a skill I excelled at. In seconds, my hands were in routine motion—one stroking my breasts, the other making lazy circles over my clit through my panties—slow, languorous circles that had my breathing quickening immediately. But what to think about? What fairy tale to display today? I stared up at the ceiling, mentally tracing a tiny crack in the biscuit-hued plaster. Not sexy. I turned my head and took in the posters on my wall: black-and-white photos of lovers kissing on the subway, kissing in a way I've never been kissed. Sexy, but distant. I'd never experienced passion like that before.

I turned my head the other way, confronted by my own image in the mirror over my dresser. Damn. Shy girl, with straight red hair, freckles, a lost look on her face.

I shut my eyes. It was safer this way.

There is a specific routine that always gets me off. I stroke myself gently at first, always through the barrier of whatever undergarments I have on.

Oh, like that. Yes, like that.

Only as the pleasure begins to build do I give in to touching myself skin to skin, fingers slipping underneath the waistband to taunt and tease. Why? I need to make myself yearn for release. See, when I'm by myself I have to play both Dom and sub.

But did I?

Suddenly I thought of Jules. He wouldn't want me to touch myself, would he? He'd want my hands tied, so that I couldn't move, so that we could see what would happen. Nice thought. But that presented an urgent problem: Could I actually come without any touching at all? Was that possible? I'd read about a porn star who could do this—a male, who would focus until he reached that pinnacle of pleasure all by himself. But, then again, he was a pro.

With my hands at my sides, I spread my legs wide on my mattress. I thought of Jules, conjuring him up in my mind.

When I draw, the pictures appear without thoughts. My hand works almost independently from my brain. I fall into the zone. That's the easiest way for me to describe the sensation.

Sometimes, when a picture is complete, I have no true recollection of having put pen to paper—or in my case, pencil to napkin. That's where most of my art takes place. I draw all the time, quick sketches or "doodles" as my co-worker Dan says, a hint of a feature here, a line of an emotion there.

Coming is like that for me. I lose myself in my fantasies. When I emerge, I am dazed.

This was different.

At first, I felt nothing. I was aroused, but I couldn't imagine climaxing without actually touching myself, physically sliding one hand down my body, pushing my fingers under my white cotton boy shorts, finding my clit and pinching tight. I tend to tease myself—throwing in firm strokes in between the sweet caresses. This was frustrating. My legs were spread, my heart was racing, but nothing happened.

I almost gave up right at the start, almost said, "fuck this" and went with the normal dog-and-pony show: round and round, in and out, round and round. A pinch, a spiral, a pinch. My hand was actually in motion, on the way back to the split of my body. But then I thought of what Sonia had written about Jules: *He said he wanted to bind me down, so that I couldn't move, and then he would see—we would see—what I had to say.*

Oh, I liked that. No man had ever spoken to me in that way. I had to steal Sonia's sex life for my own form of foreplay, but I had no shame. I stole away. What if Jules had said those words to me? How might I have responded? I definitely wouldn't have left the building. I would have desperately soaked up every last moment Jules was willing to give. So why not pretend?

My pussy began to grow wetter. I could feel my juices flowing. Slowly the heat built between my thighs. I imagined Jules watching me. I envisioned him standing at the foot of my bed, staring down at me with those dark blue eyes of his, daring me to come without any additional stimulation.

"You can do this," his eyes seemed to say.

"No, I need you. I need you to touch me," I responded, lips moving, with no sound, like a TV show on Mute.

"Come on, Kate. All you have to do is try."

"I am trying." And I was. Really.

"Try harder. Do this for me."

I'd drawn his face often enough to imagine his expression. The challenge in the tilt of his chin. The dare in his eyes.

But something was wrong. I recalled what Sonia had written in her diary, and then I brought my hands over my head and clung to the curlicues of brass that make up my headboard, pretending that I was cuffed. The metal was cold against my skin, and I shivered but didn't let go.

How could she *not* have given in to him? How could she not have said, "Yes, please"? Nothing like this had ever happened to me before.

Don't get me wrong. I'm no virgin. Maybe that's difficult to believe. Someone as shy as I am doesn't seem like a person who could land a date, much less a lay. But that's the thing. You don't need a lot of bells and whistles to find a man. I simply hadn't found the man I needed. My freshman year, I'd hooked up with a partner in my science class—but we had no true chemistry. My sophomore year, there'd been a writer I liked from my journalism class—but ultimately he was yesterday's news. Jules had always looked to me like someone I could whisper my fantasies to. The ones that kept me up after normal people went to sleep.

When you work at a café—when caffeine is freely accessible—there is no such thing as a normal time to sleep. I've grown accustomed to quietly roaming the apartment late at night, to sitting up in my window overlooking the lights of the city, to fucking myself with my vibrator while praying that one day I will find a lover who won't take my quiet surface as the end result. Who will understand sometimes the best prizes are the ones you dig to the bottom of the Cracker Jacks for.

I raised my hips. I let go of the headboard.

"Giving up so soon, Red?" Jules was displeased that I had broken the rules. His thumb stroked his belt buckle.

Resigned, I reached for the brass once more. My body was begging for release. I didn't know how much longer I could hold out. The imaginary Jules chided me. "Don't even think about letting go," he said. "I want you immobile. I want your pleasure to come at my speed. Don't make me have to punish you, Kate."

Oh, God.

"You know what I mean when I say that word, don't you?"

A shiver. A tremor.

"I can be nice and sweet, Kate. Or I can make all your filthiest dreams come true."

I let go of the headboard once more. The fantasy Jules couldn't stop me this time. *Punish.* That word always gets me off. My fingers slipped underneath the waistband of my knickers. I began to make those circles that flow as naturally from my fingertips as pictures emerge from my pencil. My hips beat against my black-and-white comforter. I shivered as the pleasure began to work through me. Hot, and wet, and stealthy.

This was ideal. The only problem was that I was all by myself. I twisted on the mattress. My fingers worked harder, faster. I bit my lip to keep from moaning, even though I was alone in an empty apartment. I felt as if Jules was really there, watching me.

You cheated, Kate, the dream Jules chided me.

Yeah, but I came, I replied, as I rolled over on the bed.

Sonia arrived home that night repeating the rules for the debate team. She entered my bedroom without knocking, as usual, and she proceeded to practice for me.

She was one of the all-star players. Sonia knew how to capture the audience's focus. I'd seen her in action often enough. She understood all the tricks. A good introduction is key. You have to grab the attention and interest of the audience from the very first line. This comes naturally to Sonia. She's a gifted debater. She knows how to state her opinion in a way that makes you think its fact. But ultimately, it's not fact. Proof? She gave me the rundown on her vegan diet with such conviction that I tried my best to follow her rules—until the tofurkey episode. That ended my vegan lifestyle with a bang.

This is what I've learned from her: a debate is a game.

There are always two different sides.

"A shot in the dark."

When Jules ordered his coffee the next morning, my hands were trembling slightly. I wondered if he noticed. Luckily I didn't spill any of the precious dark liquid, but I came close. Could he tell that I'd come the previous night while thinking of him? Jules put money down on the counter, and then he reached for a napkin. Not a fresh one from the stack, but the one I'd been drawing on. I hadn't realized he'd noticed.

"Nice cuffs, Red."

There were handcuffs in the picture.

Dan stopped going through the tip jar looking for wheat-back pennies. (He was on a quest for the 1909 S-VDB—I've heard about the penny often enough to have those numbers and letters embroiled in my brain. This particular wheatback is worth an astonishing $550. "It would make the fact that some schmuck put a penny into the tip jar so much more satisfying," he was fond of saying.) But the word "cuffs" clearly caught his interest. My picture had both wrists and cuffs. *My* wrists and cuffs.

"But you got one thing wrong," Jules said softly, eyebrows uplifted as he regarded the picture, and then looked at me. "You forgot the key-holes."

I stared down at the sketch, embarrassed, realizing he was right.

He leaned across the counter. I could feel how close we were. "How will anyone set you free if there aren't any holes for the keys?"

I blushed hot. Dan snickered behind me. I'd never seen a pair of handcuffs up close before.

Jules left a five-dollar tip in the jar, and he took the napkin with him. "Do a little research," he said over his shoulder.

I knew where the store was, a dark hole-in-the-wall type of place. These stores are never well-lit on the outside. You have to push through the dimness to find the glitter, the neon, the glow. How do I know? I had to buy my trusty vibrator somewhere. I couldn't risk having my roommate opening a delivery box from a kinky specialty catalog. I didn't know where Sonia stood on sex toys, but the thought of receiving a lecture on my pleasure wasn't something I ever hoped to experience.

Now, I wanted handcuffs. At least, I thought I did.

The shop clerk glanced up at me, gave me a quick once-over with obvious disinterest then returned to his book. He was reading at the counter, surrounded by some of the largest dildos I'd ever seen. I stared at him, the blue spiky hair, inky ribbons of tribal tattoos on his biceps. I tried to look nonchalant, but there was no way I could pull off a jaded expression. I wanted to explore everything. I wanted to touch all the toys. I wanted Jules.

"Do you have cuffs?" I asked, working for blasé, but channeling Minnie Mouse squeaky instead. Minnie Mouse on helium. Only dogs could hear me.

"Fur-lined? Regulation? Solo use?" He might have been ticking off different brands of laundry detergent. He sounded so indifferent.

I had no idea handcuffs came in multiple styles. I wished I'd paid more attention to Sonia's diary. Had she spelled out what Jules had wanted to do to her? No, she'd only said "handcuffs."

"What does 'solo use' mean?"

There was suddenly a hint of curiosity in the clerk's eyes and he closed his book. His eyes were ringed by dark kohl outlines, smudged and blurred. "You can't figure that out for yourself?" He nodded to my sweatshirt with the University logo on the center. "College girl like you?"

"I mean, how do they work?" I tried to sound like an investigative reporter. This information wasn't for me. I was simply gathering up the facts for a paper on…on…

"Ice in the lock. When the ice melts, the lock opens. You can be bound down for one hour, two, three. Depending on how much water you add to the lock, and how long you want to be immobilized." He appraised me for a moment. "But I don't believe you really can't find anyone to bind you to a bed." His apparent attraction was growing by the second.

"How do you know the cuffs are for me?" Could I trot out the line about the research paper now? Maybe I was doing a term paper on bondage devices in the twenty-first century. Or on kinky co-eds. Or on sneaky coffee vixens who read their roommates' diaries.

He smirked.

"I mean, why wouldn't you think I wanted to

bind someone else down?" Right, because I have pro-domme written all over my face. Where was this coming from? Why was I even talking to the guy?

"You have a look," he said. I thought of Sonia. Men seemed to think that *she* had a look. What kind of look did I have? "Novice, neophyte, ingé-nue," he continued, as if reading my mind.

"What's that you're reading?" I asked, feeling sarcastic. "Roget's Thesaurus?"

"You don't have to be a college boy to have a big *dick*-tionary."

"Give me all of them," I said, feeling anger rise inside of me. "Fur, regulation, solo. I want them all."

Did I? No. But I didn't want to walk out of the place empty-handed, either. The smug expression didn't leave the clerk's face as he rang up my purchases. When he handed me my change, he also handed me a card from the store. "If you can't find anyone to do the tying, angel, give me a call."

I didn't make it home before I had to come. I pulled over to the rear of a generic grocery store parking lot and shoved one hand down the front of my jeans. The need was so intense I didn't even worry about being caught. Fuck the foreplay, I crushed my fingers against my clit and rocked my hips. The pleasure was instant. I felt the wetness all over my fingertips. I took a deep breath and pressed harder still.

So I had the look of a novice. That wasn't an insult. It was the truth. But I could learn. I could be taught. I could walk up to Jules with the handcuffs in the glistening black Mylar bag and say, "Use these on me. Bind *me* down. Find out what *I* have to say."

What would I have to say?

I couldn't be sure, but I had a few ideas. I thought I might say, "Fuck me, Jules. Please fuck me." Or maybe, "Do me, baby. Oil me up and take me. Anyway you want. Anyway you like." I'd never talked like that in my life, but the thought of the cuffs unlocked a new wave of passion inside me.

A battered blue station wagon pulled next to mine, and I stopped what I was doing, frozen. Should I pull my hand out of my jeans or stay still and pretend I didn't exist? I removed my hand and reached for my satchel, rummaging through the bag as if looking for something. Something like my sanity.

What sort of rabbit hole had I fallen down? I'd walked into a sex toy store and been offered bondage. I was now in a very public location fantasizing to images of myself being cuffed by my roommate's date. A date she'd classified as *too kinky*. I had to stop. I had to get myself under control. I had to…

The middle-aged blonde driver of the car in the next spot locked her car. She had a bad dye job, I thought meanly. And her acid-washed jeans were too tight. She would never go to a sex toy store and buy three sets of handcuffs, would she? But was that an insult or praise? I watched in my rearview mirror as the woman walked toward the grocery store. I relaxed and immediately slid my hand back down my jeans. I didn't care if I was stroking myself to fantasies about Sonia's sex life. She didn't deserve a man as hot as Jules.

I squeezed my eyes shut tight and thought about the handcuffs. Thought about Jules. Wondered what he'd say if I showed up at his apartment with all three sets in the bag and asked, "Which one is right? Which one do you want?"

The problem with my fantasies was that I didn't know Jules's dialogue. I had to put words in his mouth. But I could do that.

"Let's try each one," the fantasy Jules said.

"We'll start with the steel. Cold metal on your skin. We'll bind you down, and then we'll see. I want to watch you come, Kate. I want to see your body change."

Oh, fuck, I wanted that, too.

"And then we'll try the ice lock," he continued. "I'll do my work in the other room, leave you all by yourself with your own dirty fantasies. And when I come back, you'll have to tell me each naughty one. If you don't, I'll have to punish you." A laugh. I'd heard him laugh before. But this was different. Darker. "And maybe I'll punish you anyway."

What would that mean for him? I knew what the word meant for me.

"I'll put you over my lap," Jules promised. "I'll spank you on the bare. I'm sure a spanking will make you wet. Am I right, Kate? Am I right?"

Yes. Yes, he was right.

"I'll use my hand first, and then my belt. I'll make you cry hot tears, and then I'll fuck you so hard, so fast."

My head back against the seat, my body trembling, I let the wave of pleasure slam through me and recede before I even thought about turning on the car once more.

***

At home, I spread out my new prizes on the bed. I started to manhandle each one, to stroke my fingers around the curves of the steel, to pet the fabric of the faux-fur-lined set, to investigate the ice lock. Jules had wanted to handcuff Sonia. I wanted Jules to handcuff me. But I wanted to know what handcuffs would feel like first. What if I couldn't stand the sensation of being bound down? Or what if I loved the feeling so much I never wanted any other kind of sex again?

Either way, I didn't need three pairs of cuffs. Did I?

Slowly I ran my hands over the pink, leopard-print set. These were silly—a gag gift for a bachelorette party. I would feel ridiculous wearing them. I held the steel ones. They had a good, solid weight. The keys were sweet and small. I wished I could put the cuffs on, but I was scared. What if I couldn't make the key work while my hands were bound? I put on one cuff and let the other hang loose. I liked the weight.

God, why had Jules asked Sonia out? Why hadn't he asked me?

The sound of the front door opening made me start. Quickly I tried to undo the cuff with the key, but my fingers were slippery. I climbed off my bed and kicked the door closed, the sound of soldiers marching in my head. Leaning my body weight against the door, I fumbled with the key some more. My breathing was ragged, as if I'd been running. What if Sonia came in? What if she figured out that I'd read her diary and that I wanted what she didn't want? Finally I got the key in the hole, turned the right way, released myself.

Jesus.

I shoved all the cuffs and the packaging into the bottom drawer of my battered dresser and then went out to greet Sonia. She was on the sofa, reading the rules for her next debate. "Seven minutes. First affirmative construction..."

"A shot in the dark."

When Jules bought his coffee the next day, he put his hand out.

I'd already given him his change.

"Sketch?" he asked.

Blush was apparently the new hue for me. I handed him the napkin. The cuffs had keyholes now.

"Good girl," he said before walking away. If my co-worker, Dan, hadn't been standing behind me, I would have sunk to the floor in a puddle of arousal and shame. As it was, I stared after him, hearing the words reverberate in my mind: *good girl, good girl, good girl.*

When Sonia went out the next night, I locked myself up once more. I'd been impatiently waiting for her departure for hours. In fact, I'd been so nervous and jumpy that she'd given me two separate lectures on the poison of caffeine. How could I tell her that coffee wasn't to blame for my excitable state—her diary was the culprit?

The clerk had said the ice lock would take an hour to three hours to melt depending on how much water you'd frozen. I'd gone with one hour—hiding the cuffs in the freezer behind a bag of frozen peas. I hoped I'd gone with one hour. I couldn't be entirely sure. As soon as Sonia left, I stripped off my clothes and climbed onto my bed. I fastened one cuff easily on my left wrist, and through some fairly simple maneuvers, threaded the chain through the brass curls on my headboard before attaching the other cuff to my right. Why did I get naked? Because Jules would have wanted me like that. Why did I bind myself to the headboard? That seemed the appropriately kinky thing to do.I craved knowing how this would feel—every second, every sensation. Could I come while my wrists were like this? I didn't know. So far, every time I'd tried,

I'd cheated. This would keep me from giving in.

Sonia was supposed to be at a debate club meeting. I ought to have the apartment all to myself until at least midnight.

That was the plan, anyway. But plans often go astray, especially when you are totally nude, in your bedroom, cuffed to your bed, and your roommate enters your apartment with a guest four freaking hours before you expect her home.

Holy fuck. Holy fucking fuck.

For a second, I think my heart actually stopped. Then my brain began to race with questions. Well, with the same question over and over: *What to do? What to do? What to do?* Deep down, I knew that there was nothing to do. I was cuffed—*naked* and cuffed. The chain ran through the curlicues of brass of my headboard. My heart pounded so hard I was sure Sonia could hear the throb in the living room. "What's that drum beat?" she might be asking her friend. "Is someone playing Led Zeppelin on eleven?"

Maybe she had forgotten something. She and whomever she was with would simply grab the missing item—jacket, or purse, or note cards, or Wesson Oil, whatever the fuck they'd forgotten—and be on their way. But if that was the case, then what was that sound? I didn't have to be a rocket scientist to recognize the echo of footsteps approaching down the hall, growing closer by the second.

Oh, God, why had I done this? Why hadn't I been comfortable enough with putting a single cuff on my wrist? Why had I needed to try something different?

Desperately I attempted to get free. I rattled the chain, to no avail. Maybe the heat of my cheeks would melt the ice quicker than the expected time. Nope. I bucked against the mattress.

My mind exploded with dirty words.

Sonia never knocked. Not ever. How could I not have locked the door? Simple. This was my maybe not-so-bright backup plan. I had worried that I might need assistance. What if I'd done something wrong? What if the lock got stuck? The firemen could easily open the door and find me. They wouldn't have to break down the door.

So what could I do now? Could I somehow drag the whole fucking bed through the room so I could block the door? Not likely.

The voices grew louder.

No hunky firemen were in my future. Right when I realized that I ought to simply shout out,

"Don't come in!" Sonia and Eleanor, a friend of hers from the debate team, entered my bedroom. They were talking to each other, so they did not notice me right away. That is, they didn't notice what I looked like. Then Sonia sucked in her breath, her friend looked aghast, and I bit my lip and tried hard not to cry.

The other woman politely backed out of the room—I'm sure Emily Post would have approved—but Sonia stood in the doorway, staring. Another person than I am might have been indignant. A different kind of girl might have appropriated a *what the fuck do you think you're looking at?* attitude. But that chick wasn't me.

"Are you okay?" she finally asked, her voice trembling.

"Well…" I said, thinking, "Hell, I've been better."

"Did someone do this to you?"

Sigh. *Yeah. I did. I did because I read your fucking diary, you nitwit. I did because I wanted to know what it would feel like to be handcuffed, without having to go through the whole thing of finding a boyfriend and begging him to use bondage tools on me. Men don't offer things up like this to me every day. I'm not you.*

I shook my head.

"Do you want me to unlock you or leave you alone?"

Did I really have to explain to her about the ice lock? I took a deep breath. "Don't worry about me," I said, before adding, "but maybe you could cover me up." She looked as if she didn't want to step too close to me. I wanted to tell her that I wouldn't bite, and she didn't have to worry anyway, not with me bound down. Reluctantly she came close enough to spread the quilt over my body. Then she sat at the foot of my bed and stared at me. I saw confusion in her eyes. At least, that was better than pity.

"I wanted to know," I said, as she seemed to expect some type of explanation.

"Know what?"

"What being bound would feel like."

Had she made the mathematical mental connection? Her diary plus my fantasies equaled intense orgasms.

"Well, what does it feel like?"

Wow, for once Sonia wasn't spouting platitudes at me. She wasn't telling me I should get in my light and do my work. She wasn't explaining the dangers of kinky sex. Instead she looked truly interested in what I had to say.

I stammered, "I like the sensation." I'd have liked it a whole lot better if Jules had been between my thighs, but I kept that part to myself.

Nothing happened after that. I waited until I could free myself, and then I freed myself. There was no way I was going to get off tonight. I was so mortified that I didn't even leave my bedroom until I was sure that Sonia's guest had departed and Sonia had gone to sleep. Except, as I was brushing my teeth, I thought I heard soft noises from Sonia's room. Noises I'd never heard before. These weren't the sounds of a heated debate.

Not unless a heated debate sounds a lot like fucking.

"Oh, God," I heard in a stagelike whisper, then louder, "Oh, my, God!"

I paused, and then realized my electric toothbrush was still running. Quickly I pressed the button to turn off the brush. I wanted to hear everything I possibly could. Sonia's normally recognizable voice sounded extremely unrecognizable. There was lust, passion, arousal in her moans.

Should I come closer? Press myself up to her door and try to peek? No. I'd been caught by her already today. I didn't want to flip the situation and catch her. Still, I couldn't wait to read her diary the next day.

But when I went to look in the morning, the book wasn't there.

Jules strolled up to the coffee bar as usual. I started trembling when he approached the counter to order. "Shot in the dark, right?"

He reached out and put a hand on top of mine, holding me still, calming me down. Was he going to ask to see more of my sketches? I had a stack behind the counter. Was he going to tell me he'd only threatened Sonia with cuffs as a joke?

"Everyone knows she's a lesbian," Jules said, smiling.

I couldn't believe what he was saying. "Break," I told Dan, "be right back." Dan gave me the evil eye before stepping up to the counter. He liked making money, but he hated having to work. I walked out of the small structure to find Jules waiting for me at the back.

"What did you say?"

He took my hand again. I was extremely aware of his skin against my skin. I wanted to tell him that usually, I touch myself through a barrier. Only when the heat arises do I try skin on skin.

To mimic this in real life, we ought to have been wearing gloves. Those were the nervous, crazy thoughts jangling through my brain. Luckily I was wise enough to keep my lips sealed as he led me away from the coffee bar, down a little hill, to a concrete planter. We sat together under a jacaranda tree. All around us were the pale, purple blossoms, the honeyed scent in the air. Maybe this was a dream. I couldn't, for the life of me, understand what was happening.

"Sonia's a lesbian. You know that. I know that."

"She doesn't know that," I said. Then I backtracked. "Well, I mean, I don't think she did until last night."

"What happened last night, Red?" He stroked my hair out of my eyes, and a fresh tremor ran through me. He was gazing at me in a way that men generally admired Sonia. Which reminded me in a heartbeat that he'd asked her out first.

"I think she hooked up with Eleanor. But why on earth did you ask her out if you think she's into women?"

He stared at me with the same expression I'd seen on his face in class, a look that said he knew something more than the instructor did, had a concept that had yet to be explained.

"You really can't guess?"

I shook my head.

"You can, but you want me to say the words. That's fine. I can say the words. I asked her out because I wanted you…"

"But…" I wanted to believe him. My heart felt too big in my chest. He had his hands on my wrists now. I gave a test tug, pulling. He held on tight. *Handcuffs.* I saw that word again—this time written in my mind instead of in Sonia's notebook.

"But why didn't I ask you out from the start?"

I swallowed hard and nodded.

"I wanted you to *want* what I was going to give you. I wanted you to be consumed with need. There are rules in a debate," he said, "but there are always people who cheat."

Oh, Christ. He'd played me so well. Knowing how jealous I was of how men responded to her, knowing somehow that I was kinky. How had he known that? How had he known I wanted someone to tie me up?

"But what if she'd said yes?" I needed to know the answer to this.

"She wasn't going to say yes."

"What if she had?"

He shrugged. The lady or the tiger? I would have to choose the decision for myself. Would he have postponed the encounter, or tied her up and fucked her? Did either answer make me want to run? No.

I stopped tugging. His grip did not relax. He squeezed even tighter, before finally releasing me.

"Do you know where I live?" he asked.

I nodded without telling him I'd stood outside his apartment before, staring up at his windows. Considering begging him to handcuff me.

"Come to my place after work," he said.

He would have no debate from me.

I burned myself twice in the next two hours. Exasperated, Dan finally told me to call it a day. I must really have been driving him nuts if he were willing to man the coffee shack by himself. I untied the apron and grabbed up my battered messenger bag. I knew I ought to go home and change clothes—the aroma of coffee permeated my whole being. I could go and snag one of Sonia's little dresses from her closet, put some emphasis on my figure, something different from my standard uniform of faded jeans and a plain white button-down.

But when I went to her room and looked in her

closet, I was at a loss. How could I put on a costume when all I really wanted was for Jules to see me naked? I headed back to my room. At the very least, I could capture my hair in a flirty ponytail. I might even slick on my one shade of lip gloss, if I could find the tube.

On my bed sat a book—a book I recognized immediately. Sonia's diary. That's why I hadn't found the journal in the morning. She'd cottoned on to the fact that I was a snoop. Guilt flickered through my body. That didn't stop me from perching on the edge of my mattress and cracking the spine once more. Her latest entry was written differently this time. It was written directly to me.

When I saw you on your bed like that, I couldn't get the image out of my mind. I went and told Eleanor what I'd seen, and Eleanor spoke to me differently than anyone ever had. Do you want that? she asked me. Want... She hesitated.

To be tied down, or tied up?

It's no coincidence, is it? You read my diary. You saw what he said. You knew what he did.

The guilt was back. I was shivering all over.

But I'm not angry, Kate. Because last night with Eleanor was the best fucking night I ever had. The best night fucking, too.

Now, I smiled.

Oh, yeah. And do you think we could borrow your cuffs sometime?

I put down Sonia's diary and grabbed the pretty faux-fur, leopard-print cuffs from my bottom drawer. She'd like these best, I thought. They went with her style. I set both the cuffs and key and diary on Sonia's bed. Then I looked at my clock. Jules had said to meet him after work. Maybe I ought to have changed—turned myself into someone else. Like in one of those fairy tales I used to read when I was a kid. But I didn't have a godmother.

Instead I went as myself.

Jules was waiting for me on his front porch, beer in hand.

I could hardly speak English when he opened the front door for me. I might have said Hello but the word was erased by the sound of a truck rumbling by on the road, and I didn't try again. Jules waited like a gentleman for me to step inside and came in after me. Was I really here? Was this really happening? I turned to look at Jules. He smiled, as if he could read all the thoughts that were in my head. But he couldn't possibly. There was no way that he could know how often I'd thought about him, and the dirty things I'd imagined him doing to me.

He set his beer down on the table in the entryway. I set my satchel down on the floor. We stared at each other for a moment, and I wondered if this was going to be easy or awkward or…

"This way."

Easy. I let him lead me once more, this time to the bedroom. I thought of Sonia, thought of her hot-tempered reaction to his initial suggestion. How different I was, meek and willing, desperate.

"You look in the mirror," he said when we got to his room, "but you don't see the truth."

"What do you mean?" His room was all white. White walls, white furniture. But the bed had a black spread on the mattress, and there were framed black-and-white posters on the walls. I was secretly thrilled to see several that I owned, as well.

"You don't see. You can't possibly. Or you wouldn't behave the way you do." As if to prove his point, he spun me around, so I was facing a gilded oval mirror hanging above his bed. I looked down. He tilted my chin up. I shut my eyes. He brought his mouth to my ear and said, "Don't disobey me. If I want your eyes closed, I'll use a blindfold."

His words made me instantly wet. Did he know? Could he tell?

I sucked my lower lip between my teeth and bit hard. I wished I could be eloquent with words the way Sonia was, able to put arguments into clean, precise phrases. Able to fight when someone tried to dispute me. Not that I wanted to fight Jules, but I wanted to understand, and I wanted to be able to voice my…my…fears.

"I watched you in class. You soak up everything, but you don't respond. And then I realized, it's all in there. You keep your emotions within, sublime and tight. You don't know how to let things out."

"So you're going to tie me down to teach me how to let go?" There. That was a little voice, right? Jules smiled again. God, he had a nice smile.

"She's learning. Quick, too. That's not all I'm going to do, Kate."

Had he said my name before? Like that? Outside of my fantasies? I didn't think so. He'd always called me Red. I wanted to hear him say it again. *Please, say Kate again*, I silently willed.

"What else are you going to do?" And how had I gotten myself backed into a corner like this?

Somehow, I had managed to wedge myself completely into one corner of Jules's bedroom. My arms were crossed over my chest, and my hands rested on my shoulders as if I were trying to mimic a mummy in a sarcophagus.

"What do you want me to do, Kate?"

Oh, like that. The way he said my name struck a chord within me. I wanted him to press his lips to my ear and whisper my name over and over. Instead of telling him this, I shrugged, feeling the walls on both sides. He was waiting. Clearly waiting. Finally I whispered, "I want you to do what you said."

"What I said to who?"

I sucked in my breath. "I read Sonia's diary," I confessed. "I want you to do to me what you said you'd do to her."

I didn't have to ask him twice.

He had cuffs like the second pair I'd purchased: regulation, steel handcuffs with a silver gleam. I knew what they were going to feel like. I'd held them. Cradled them. Caressed them. None of that prepared me for the sensation of having Jules strip me of my clothes and position me in the center of his bed. I thought I'd been so smart doing the research, buying the toys. Turned out, I hadn't learned a fucking thing.

"Arms over your head." I was naked on his mattress, and I felt his warm hands on my wrists before the cold steel closed tight.

I took a breath. I could come from this alone, I thought. Why had I needed to cheat every other night? Simple. Because Jules hadn't been in the room.

He stared down at me, and his face looked different than all of my sketches. "You bought the cuffs when I told you to do research, didn't you, Kate?"

"Yes."

What had been missing from my drawings? The warmth in his eyes that I saw now. He was handsome, yes, but he was more than that. He looked pleased with me, as if I'd risen to some challenge.

"And you tried them out?"

I thought of the fiasco with Sonia walking in, and I turned my head away from his. He gripped my chin and forced me to meet his gaze. "When I want you to look away from me, I'll tell you," he said. There was a beat of menace to his voice. But that made me wetter still.

"Yeah, I tried them," I admitted.

"That's what she told me."

"She?" The words weren't making sense.

"I was helping her prepare for her debate. She told me that she'd found you."

"I thought she was never going to talk to you again."

He shrugged. "There's *never* and then there's *never*. After she got together with Eleanor, she called and wanted to talk."

"So she told you…" He'd known the answer before he'd asked the question.

He grinned. "I would have liked to have found you like that. Walked in. Discovered you bound to your bed all by yourself. The games I could have played with you."

I would have turned my head away, but he'd told me not to. I would have shut my eyes, tried to hide my embarrassment, but he'd already warned me. Instead I simply stared back at him, forced to face my fears. My stomach tightened. This was much more difficult than I'd expected.

"Good girl," he said, just as he had before, words that warmed me inside as if he'd banked my internal furnace. "Don't turn away from me. Don't ever turn away from me."

Then it was like every fantasy I've ever had and ones I never thought of before. He started by kissing me, his lips on mine, kissing hard. I'd been kissed by other men—but maybe what I'd

felt previously should be given a different name
from kissing. Those were pecks. Smooches. This
was real. This was what kissing is all about, a defi-
nition from a dirty dictionary. I felt his lips part
against mine. I felt our tongues meet. I wanted this
to go on forever, at least until he slid one hand
along my body and began to stroke my pussy.

"You're wet," he said.

"I know."

That changed everything. Now, I wanted
something else, something new, something more.
Jules began to kiss his way down my body. He
didn't leave any part untouched. If his mouth
was caressing my nipples—one, then the other—
then his hands were busy stroking and fondling
every inch of my skin. I felt beloved, admired,
adored.

And still I wanted more.

Greedy. That's what I was. Jules didn't seem to
mind.

Finally he slid between my legs and parted my
pussy lips. "Oh, God," I sighed, unable to keep
quiet.

"Go on," he said, "make noise. Let it out.
When I want you quiet, I'll use a gag."

I hadn't gone there mentally before. A gag. A
ball gag? A leather strip? Would I have to make

another trip to the sex toy store? Maybe. But I had the feeling I wouldn't have to go there alone. I imagined what the tattooed, wise-ass clerk would think if I walked into the place with Jules at my side, and then I fell back into reality as he started to lick my clit. For once reality was better than my fantasies. Jules knew exactly how to work me. He seemed to understand how sensitive I was, and he began slowly. But he didn't stay slow for long.

"You like that?"

I looked down at him. His lips were glossy with my own juices. That realization brought a fresh tremor of excitement throughout me, and I bucked on the bed as a way of answering. Jules was having none of that. "Answer me when I ask you a question," he murmured.

"Yes," I told him. "Yes, I like that."

He made sensuous circles with the point of his tongue. Then, "Tell me. Tell me what you like."

I couldn't believe it. He actually wanted me to speak at a moment like this?

"Tell me, Kate."

"Everything," I said, hoping that would satisfy him, but knowing somehow that it wouldn't.

"Tell me exactly."

"What you're doing," I stammered. "The way you're making those circles."

Oh, it felt so good. He spiraled his tongue in circles that grew smaller and smaller until he was focused right on my clit. The pleasure and the pressure were intense. I would have pulled away, but I couldn't. Not handcuffed like that. Was that the point? I'd always thought of bondage as something you did in a dungeon—an atmosphere of darkness and chill pervading. But this was all heat and wet. I rattled the chain. He licked me harder.

Fuck, that felt good. As soon as I thought the words, I said them out loud. "Fuck, that feels good." My voice had become the blending of a moan and a sigh. Jules continued, bringing me higher and higher until I could almost taste the bliss of the impending climax.

Then he stopped.

I would have done anything, said anything, promised anything for him to continue. But he backed off the bed and went to his desk. He returned with a stack of white paper squares, paper I recognized, napkins I'd drawn on. He showed me the pictures, one by one, and I felt my cheeks burn. Now I did look away. Jules's tone made me turn back to him.

"You told me what you wanted," he said, "without ever saying a word."

"But why…?" I was in that hazy state of almost coming, yet I still needed to ask. "Why?"

"I told you before. If I'd just asked you out, you'd have been nervous and jittery. Unsure. You might have run away when I told you the things I hoped to do to you. Instead you came looking. You came to me."

"Where'd you get the napkins?"

"Dan."

I thought about my mercenary co-worker. Before I could ask the next question, Jules said, "A dollar a napkin. He's been saving them for me."

He stripped off his own clothes and then crawled back on the mattress. We were surrounded by my pictures, drawings of people fucking, of couples overlapping, of handcuffs, and blindfolds and toys. There was him. There was me.

Jules moved up my body and parted my legs. I could not wait for him to thrust inside me. My whole being was poised on the edge of that precipice. Was he going to tease me some more? Make me beg? Demand I tell him exactly what was running through my mind? Thankfully, no. He slid the head of his cock inside me, and I sighed and relaxed. Oh, this was sweetness. This was heaven and light. And then he started to move, pounding into me, thrusting hard. I had never felt anything like this. I was captured by the cuffs, but my body could still respond, my hips raised to meet his, my thighs spread apart. He used one hand to touch me, running his palm over my ribs, over the flat of my belly, then down to my pussy.

"Oh, yes," I hissed. "Just like that."

Lust bloomed bright within me.

As he fucked me, he stroked my clit, light and easy at first, then rougher as the passion built between us. I shut my eyes tight, but he said, "No, Kate, look at me." And then, "Please, Kate. For me." Surprising me because he sounded almost as if he were the one begging.

I opened my eyes. I stared at him.

We were connected, bound together somehow, even as I was the one bound down. The handcuffs rattled as he thrust inside of me, reminding me with every beat that I was his captive. And yet somehow, somehow, I felt as if we'd set each other free.

How neatly our bodies fit together. I'd never paused to wonder, to worry, whether we'd be compatible. If his parts would interlock with my parts. Thankfully they did. Perfectly. His cock seemed made for my body. Each time he drove forward, I felt my muscles contract, as if wanting to hold him to me forever. My hands were useless, but I possessed plenty of other powers. My legs around his body, pulled him to me.

Jules used his thumb right against my clit as he fucked me, finding a rhythm that made sense— the rhythm of my blood, of my heart, or maybe of our hearts beating together. We were in complete synch. He worked me steadily, and I kept our connection solid, gazing into his deep blue eyes—the color of cobalt, rich and dark. Even as I wanted to hide, even as the pleasure became almost insurmountable, I kept staring into his eyes. Seeing him. Really seeing him. How was he doing this? How did he know?

"I'm going to…" I gasped, teetering right on the cusp.

"Yes, yes," he said. "Come for me, Kate. Come *with* me."

The climax was different from any I'd ever had. Better. Beautiful. I felt electrified, as if every single part of my body was coming at the same time, as if I were all lit up with fairy lights. Jules bucked hard inside me, fucking me so hard I felt the bed shake. Then he stilled, his strong arms coming tight around my body, his cheek pressed to my cheek.

"I found you," he said. "You showed me the keyholes. I had the key."

I realized he was right. He'd played me.

And we'd won.

The Envelope Incident

By Emelia Elmwood

Emelia Elmwood fell in love with the romance genre in high school, when she picked up a dog-eared copy of Jude Deveraux's The Conquest at a friend's house. She discovered her passion for women's erotica while researching a paper for her women's studies class in college.

A Midwestern girl at heart, Emelia spent several years on the West Coast before admitting she was most at home on the Plains. She's a local-history junkie, loves reading recipes but rarely cooks and stays up way too late most nights.

Emelia and her husband live in the heart of America with their menagerie of animals and houseplants.

My two best guy friends, Jake and Derek, came over that Saturday morning to cheer me up. I poured three cups of fresh coffee and set out a plate of danishes, a sinful treat in honor of my being dumped by Stephen, my boyfriend of three years.

Neither Jake nor Derek had the decency to look as if they felt bad for me.

"What you need," Jake said, as he chewed on a cheese danish, "is to purge him from your system."

"I could start drinking," I said. "That oughtta flush him right out."

Derek shook his head. "No, something more…dramatic, I think."

"Take a trip?" I suggested. "Maybe some sort of spiritual journey? Or a weekend at a health spa?"

Jake and Derek were my very gay next-door

neighbors who had adopted me minutes after I'd left Oklahoma for a job in Los Angeles. Jake was a lawyer at a nonprofit organization downtown. Derek was an amazing hair stylist at an upscale salon in Hollywood. The two of them had become the brothers I'd never had. Plus, I now had really great hair.

"I've been thinking about this for a while now," Jake said. "I think that in order for you to find happiness in the next relationship, to rectify the karma, so to speak, you need to identify the single most problematic element of your relationship with Stephen and deal with it. Otherwise, you might just end up with another Stephen."

I sipped my coffee and thought about that for a moment. "Are you sure I only have to identify one problem? It seems like I could make a list."

Derek reached for a second danish. "If you really think about it, all of the other problems were just, I don't know, symptoms of the main one. Secondary problems."

I looked at Derek. "It sounds as though you've already identified the primary problem."

"Come on, Emma." Derek gave me a pleading look. "Think."

I didn't know where to start. Stephen and I

seemed to be pretty matched personality-wise. We both loved movies, hiking, traveling, reading, Mexican food.

"This is just pathetic," Jake said. "Either you're absolutely clueless, or too embarrassed to admit the problem."

I looked up.

"Sex," Derek said. "You were sexually incompatible."

"I take offense to that," I said. "The sex was fine."

"Was it? He always looked a heck of a lot cheerier when he left in the morning than you did when you left in the morning."

I blushed. There was something weird about knowing your two gay brother stand-ins were tracking your sexual progress.

"Here's what I think," Jake said. "I think that Stephen pursued you because he saw you as a cute, all-American good girl from Oklahoma. Which isn't a bad thing." He held up a hand before I could protest. "But you also have a pretty serious inner tigress who likes adventure. And when you figured out that he might be scared off by the inner tigress, you caged her up."

"The problem, as I see it," Derek added, "is that Stephen picked up on the fact that you were holding something back from him, and that you weren't happy. And that's why he walked."

"And now you're worried that I'm going to keep my inner tigress locked up," I said, my eyebrows raised. "That's just weird, guys."

"Is it? What if, deep down, you're really worried that he picked up on that inner tigress? What if you think you just have to work harder to keep her caged up? You'll never be happy. The men you're with will never be happy. And then we'll never be happy," Jake said. "And you don't want us unhappy, right?"

I leaned back in my chair and nursed my coffee cup. This conversation was getting a little embarrassing for my all-American good-girl self. "So what's the cure?"

"A week of hot sexual escapades that will purge the lame missionary sex with Stephen right out of your soul," Derek said.

I burst into laughter.

"Uh, with whom?" I was laughing so hard that my coffee was sloshing over the rim of my cup. "You guys?"

"I love you to bits, Emma, but you're just not my type," Jake said. "But we know a lot of guys—and a few girls, too—who would totally dig you."

I looked back and forth from Jake to Derek. "You're serious."

"Totally," Derek said.

"No fucking way," I said.

Jake pressed the back of his hand to his head in mock horror. "The inner tigress surfaced to utter a foul word, Derek."

"No," I said.

"You don't even know what we were going to say," Jake said.

"I don't have to. I don't think this is a good idea," I said. "Besides, I don't need your opinion of me to sink. I feel low enough all on my own right now."

Derek leaned forward on his arms and gave me the most serious look I've ever seen from him. "Sweetheart, there is nothing that we'd like more than to see you be comfortable with yourself. How could we think less of you for that? Especially a couple of guys like us?"

Both Derek and Jake were estranged from their families because they were openly gay. Derek's father, a man who preached "love everyone" from the pulpit, had given Derek the boot when he'd turned eighteen. Jake's family had tried at first to be understanding, but when his nieces and nephews were born, Jake had grown tired of the way his sisters shielded their children from him. So he'd faded away.

I'd never really thought about how hard that must have been, leaving family and friends like that. Yet I couldn't imagine Derek and Jake happy had they not been true to themselves.

"You think it will take a whole week, huh?"

"Look," Jake said, "here's what I think you should do." He reached behind him to the kitchen counter, where I kept a pad of paper and pens near my cell-phone charger. "Ask your inner tigress to name the three most daring things she would like to try. Three things that she's almost too embarrassed to even tell you about. Write them down, one to each piece of paper. Put them in an envelope and slip them under our door. We'll make it happen for you."

I could only sit there and blink. "You've got to be kidding me," I said.

"Think about it," Derek said. He and Jake kissed my cheeks and headed out the door.

I refused to think about it. I cleaned my apartment. No, I scoured my apartment. I went for a walk. Then I tried jogging. Then I rented a half-dozen movies. Two weeks passed, and I was restless, frustrated, embarrassed.

Then the dreams started. Very, very sexy

dreams. I was tied up and naked and hands roamed my body. I was bent over a chair while being pounded by a giant cock. Mouths sucked on my nipples. Streams of cum shot across my chest.

For three nights in a row, I woke up hot, wet, sweating, needing. Pushing myself over the edge wasn't enough. I wanted more.

At three-thirty on a Wednesday morning, I sat at my kitchen table and picked up the pen and pad of paper with shaking hands.

Images of my dreams flashed through my mind. Even though I sat alone in my kitchen, my cheeks flushed with embarrassment. A good girl didn't have thoughts like this. A good girl didn't sit at her kitchen table, thinking about what kinds of crazy sex she secretly dreamed of having with people she didn't even know.

What the hell is the matter with me? I thought. *I'm just writing down thoughts. I don't even have to show them to anyone. I can have fantasies. I can write them down.*

I held my pen over the paper, poised to write.

It was four-fifteen, and I still hadn't written a single word.

When did I become such a coward?

Or is the problem that I couldn't narrow my

list down to three? I giggled. *Gee, Jake*, I could picture myself saying, *I hope you don't mind that I gave you thirty-five different pieces of paper. I hope you have that many friends.*

Just write something, I said to myself. *Anything. The first thing that comes to your mind.*

I took a deep breath and wrote in the most honest tone I could muster:

I want to be tied up, blindfolded and fucked by men I don't know and will never see.

My heart raced so hard I could feel the pulse in my throat. With a shaky hand, I reached for a second piece of paper from the pad.

I want to taste pussy.

I couldn't believe I wrote that. I was so hot and so wet just thinking about it. I reached for a third piece of paper and thought about what my very last sexual fantasy might be.

I want two men at once. I want to ride a big cock while another cock is riding my ass.

I threw the pen on the table and jumped out of the chair. Tears of embarrassment streamed down my face, but I was so hot, so turned on, that I lay down on my living room floor and fingered myself into three orgasms before I was calm enough to sleep.

***

I slipped the envelope under Jake and Derek's door, hoping no one saw me do it. During the entire six-mile drive to work, which took a solid forty-three minutes in Los Angeles traffic, emotions tumbled around in my head. I couldn't believe I had actually written down three fantasies. I couldn't believe I'd shared them with Jake and Derek. God, what were they going to think when they saw them? What were they going to do? What would my landlord think when a bunch of random people started visiting my apartment, and the oh-so-obvious sounds of wild sex could be heard through the walls?

I almost rear-ended the car in front of me twice.

And yet I was so, so very wet.

After work, I all but tiptoed back to my apartment. I just couldn't face Jake and Derek after what I was beginning to think of as The Envelope Incident. Relieved to go undetected, I locked the apartment's deadbolt and headed to the kitchen for a glass of water. My cell phone chimed its three-tone notice of a new text message. It was from Derek.

Biltmore downtown. 8 p.m. tonite. Rm 436.

Holy shit. That was only two hours from now.

Jake and Derek knew me well enough to know

that I would look for a chicken exit if they gave me time to find one. They weren't going to give me much of a chance to back out.

I showered and headed for the Biltmore.

I found the elevator and pressed Four. I stepped into the hallway and followed the arrows to 436. I stood in front of the door for what seemed like forever. I thought about walking away. I thought about running away. But then I thought about how one of my very own fantasies was supposed to be on the other side of that door. The hallway was empty. Who would know that I had been here? Who would know about this indulgence?

My inner tigress knocked on the door.

A tall, elegant woman with blue eyes and dark hair swept up into a knot answered the door. "I'm Evie," she said. "I'm here to help you get ready."

The room was actually a posh suite. We stood in the foyer, which led to a large living room. Across the room were French doors, presumably leading to the bedroom.

Evie took my hand and led me to the guest bathroom. She helped me undress and then gave me a lacy black robe to wear. I looked at myself in the mirror, my dark blond hair, my gray eyes, my pretty decent country-girl figure that was a little curvier and rounded than was preferred in Los Angeles. I felt self conscious and insecure.

Evie ran her eyes over what she could see through the robe. I felt a flash of heat as the approval registered on her face. "Jake was right," she said. "Nate and Alex will love you."

She led me across the living room and opened one of the French doors to the bedroom. Two incredibly hot men were inside—one sitting on the giant California-King-size bed, the other sitting in an armchair. Both men wore black robes. The men stood as I entered the room.

"This is Emma," Evie said. She untied the sash of my robe and, stepping behind me, pulled it off. "She's all yours." Evie let the robe pool on the floor before stepping out of the room and closing the door behind her.

I stood there, naked and somewhat in shock, unsure of what to do. The blond man who had been sitting on the bed walked over to me and traced a finger from my chin down past my collar bone to the valley between my breasts. He was at least a foot taller than me, tanned, muscular and blue-eyed. I was wet just from looking at him.

"I'm Nate," he said. "Jake thought Alex and I could take extra special care of you."

Alex walked over to us and stood to my left. He traced my spine from my hairline down to my ass with the fingers of his right hand. Alex had an olive complexion, dark hair and dark eyes, and though he was a couple of inches shorter than Nate, he was just as muscular.

"So perfect," Alex murmured. "Just like Jake promised."

I looked each man in the eye. They were serious.

"So what do we do now?" I whispered.

"Now we satiate your tigress," Nate whispered back, and put his lips on mine. They were both soft and hard, and oh so perfect. I opened my mouth and let his tongue slide inside. I put one hand inside the opening of his robe, and he let go of me just long enough to shed it. His hands stroked my arms, and though my eyes were closed, I memorized the feel of his chest, his arms, followed the trail of hair down his chest, and brushed against his hot, velvety smooth cock.

I almost came on the spot.

Alex stood behind me, his teeth and tongue gliding and scraping along my neck. Shivers rippled over my skin. Nate fell to his knees before me and took my right nipple into his mouth. Alex held me up as I nearly crumpled with a moan.

I ran my hands through Nate's hair as he sucked and nibbled on my tits. *Yes, tits*, I thought. *This is just too hot to think good and proper words. Tonight was about getting fucked.*

My inner tigress growled with approval.

As he tugged on my left nipple with his teeth, his hand moved between my legs.

"God, you're ready," he said, almost in wonder. He rubbed his fingers over my clit, watched the syrupy wetness string from my pussy to his lips as he tasted his fingers. He pushed two fingers deep inside me. I was on the brink of an earth-shattering orgasm when I felt Alex gently spread my ass cheeks apart. Kneeling behind me, he ever-so-gently licked that most-delicate spot.

My control shattered and I came, holding on to Nate to keep from falling over.

"Now," Nate said. He stood and led me to the bed. He grabbed a condom off of the nightstand and rolled it down the length of his cock. He threw a second one to Alex, who did the same thing.

Nate lay down on the bed, his legs hanging over the end.

"Climb on top of me, Emma," he said. Mesmerized, I straddled him, facing him, my hands on his chest, my pussy rubbing over the head of his cock. He held it in place. "Now," he said, and I slid down the length of cock until my lips were pressed against his skin. He moaned as my muscles stroked and squeezed him.

"God, don't move," he said. "Just lean forward a little."

I tilted toward him, let him cup my tits in his hands. He tugged at my nipples. "Does that feel good, Emma?" he asked as I moaned. "Do you want me to play harder?" His cock inside me pulsed and I moaned again. "Tell me, Emma. Tell me what you want."

"Yes," I said. "I love it when you're rough with them." He squeezed my breasts and pulled harder on my nipples. Electricity shot from my tits to my clit.

Behind me, Alex was pouring lube over his fingers. "Just relax," he whispered, and gently rubbed my asshole with cool, wet strokes. My skin was on fire. I didn't know if I was going to last long enough to get to the final deed. Nate's cock pulsed inside me.

"Have you ever done this before?" Alex asked.

"Only myself, with a dildo," I admitted.

"Tell me what you liked about it," he told me, his fingers still feather-light, dancing around my still-tight sphincter.

I moaned.

"Tell me," he said again. "Tell me why you want a cock in your ass."

"God," I said, "it feels so good to be…full. It feels so good to be stretched to the point of it hurting. It turns me on to think about it being a cock, holding me open like that.…" I sobbed with pleasure as he slipped a finger into my ass. He worked it in and out. The walls of my pussy pulsed around Nate's cock, which pulsed in response.

"More," I said to Alex. "I want more." Doing my bidding, Alex slipped in another finger.

"I love the way you're opening up for me," he said, and slipped in a third finger.

"Please," I begged, "I can't wait anymore."

"Tell us what you want, Emma," Nate commanded from beneath me. "Tell us what you want us to do to you right now."

"God, Alex, please," I begged. "Please. I want your cock deep inside me. I want you moving in me. I want to ride Nate. I just want you both to fuck me. Now. Please!"

Alex stood between Nate's knees and pushed

his long, hard cock into my ass. I stifled a scream as he invaded my ass, pushed deep inside me. I felt so hot, so full... Alex moved in long, steady strokes, which slid me up and down the length of Nate's cock. I was sure I would be torn to pieces.

Alex's hands roamed my back as Nate and I kissed. The blood roared in my head. I couldn't think. I could barely breathe. At any moment I was going to shatter—closer, closer, closer to the edge, until I finally let my body go, felt my ass and my pussy squeezing, gripping both cocks hard and fast as I thrashed with the most intense orgasm I'd ever had. Nate grabbed my hips and gave a hard thrust, and I felt his head spasm inside me. Then Alex gripped my hips hard and with three more quick strokes, shouted with his own orgasm.

I collapsed on top of Nate.

Alex collapsed on top of me.

For a moment, the only sound in the room was that of rapid breathing, slowly calming down.

"Ready?" Alex asked. I nodded. He slowly pulled himself out of my ass. I gasped at how empty I suddenly felt.

"Your turn," Nate said, and I lifted my body off Nate's cock.

I thought it would be awkward once we were

finished. But it wasn't awkward. I felt strong and fulfilled and thrilled.

Nate wrapped my robe around me as he kissed me. "You're a treasure, Emma," he said. He turned me towards the double French doors. "Evie's waiting for you."

Two evenings later, I received another text message, this time from Jake.

Tigress – Omni downtown. Rm 1605. 9 p.m.

I wondered which of the two remaining fantasies it would be this time. I also wondered what I would owe Jake and Derek for their expensive taste in hotels. I took the elevator to the sixteenth floor, more excited than nervous this time, ready for my prize on the other side of the door to room 1605.

I knocked. Evie answered the door.

"The others will be here soon," Evie said. "I'll help you get ready."

Evie led the way to a luxurious bathroom complete with a sunken marble tub and shower with multiple shower heads. Without asking, she pulled the zipper down the back of my dress, trailing her fingers down my back.

"Too bad I'm not your fantasy tonight," she murmured. The dress fell to the floor, and I unclasped my bra and pulled off my thong. Evie held up my attire for the night—a teddy with cutouts for the tits and an open crotch.

"Wow," I said, as I stood in front of the mirror admiring the teddy. Hell, even I wanted to have sex with myself in that outfit.

I followed Evie to the giant four-poster bed. A black eye mask lay on a pillow, and sets of velvet cuffs were attached to the posts with long silky ropes. My heart pounded even faster.

"Why so many cuffs?" I asked Evie.

She smiled at me knowingly. "It depends on what they decide to do with you," she said. "But I have specific instructions regarding your first fuck of the night. Lie on your back across the bed."

Evie wrapped a cuff around each wrist and each ankle. I was spread-eagled across the width of the bed, my tits exposed, air swirling around my open crotch. Evie fitted the mask over my eyes, the elastic around my head. She ran a hand from my collarbone to my crotch. My nipples hardened and my pussy grew wet from her touch.

"I'll be back to get you ready for round two," she said, and quietly left the room.

A few minutes later, I heard the door open

and close. Heavy footsteps approached the bed. There was a rustle of fabric—maybe a robe coming off?—and then I jerked against my restraints when large hands groped my tits.

"Perfect," a man said in a gruff voice. His hands were a worker's hands, coarse and rough and strong. He kneaded my tits deliciously hard, making them ache with need. I felt a heavy thigh on each side of my chest and realized he was straddling my body. Something hard, hot and velvety brushed my lips. His cock.

"Lick," he ordered in a rumbling bass. I licked and swirled my tongue over this cock I could not see. He rubbed his cock over the exposed parts of my face, my neck, my tits. He crawled down my body, his heavy meat searing my skin through the lace of the teddy as it rubbed over my chest, stomach and thighs. My legs were spread wide, and as my pussy grew wetter, I was increasingly aware of how exposed I was. I gasped when his rough, foreign fingers probed into my wet snatch.

Man Number One murmured his approval as he rubbed the head of his cock in my juices. He lifted my ass with his rough hands and thrust his cock into me in one hard stroke. I screamed from the invasion, the pure ecstasy of it. He moved in long, deliberate strokes, holding my hips up so that I could feel each deep thrust in my core. I could feel the orgasm coming, I wanted to squeeze him closer to me and control him, but the velvet cuffs held firm and all I could do was scream with the sensitivity following the orgasm as he continued to control the rhythm of our movements. I came again, and he pulled out.

I felt him climb up my body again, his thighs straddling my ribs, his knees in my armpits.

"Taste yourself," he ordered, and I licked my own juices off of his cock. Sweet and salty. Warm and wet.

"Open your mouth," he said, and he pushed part of his shaft and head into my mouth. I suckled and licked, and he moved his cock in and out of my mouth with a gentle but determined rhythm. His cock jerked out of my mouth, and streams of cum poured over my lips and down my neck. Man Number One climbed off me. I heard the rustle of fabric and the door opened and closed.

His cum was still warm on my neck when I heard Evie chuckling. I felt a warm, wet cloth pass over my neck and face and between my legs. Then Evie uncuffed me, and told me to lie on my stomach lengthwise on the bed. She recuffed me, one limb to each bedpost, and left the room.

Man Number Two entered the room, and I heard the familiar rustle of fabric. The room grew silent, and I felt nervous when I realized he was probably studying me from somewhere in the room. He must have been standing at the foot of the bed, because two large hands slipped under the back of my teddy and kneaded my ass.

"I have something special in mind for you," he said in a smooth, silky baritone. He pulled his hands away and I heard sounds I couldn't readily identify. Then I felt fingers prying the thin thong of the teddy away from my asshole. A cold, smooth and slippery object rubbed delicious circles over my puckered hole. My whole body coursed with excitement, my pussy wet, wondering what Man Number Two was going to do.

"Relax," he whispered. "I want to see your asshole swallow this butt plug."

I willed myself to open up to his toy, and was rewarded with the slurping sound of the smooth object being pulled into me. I sighed happily as my sphincter gripped the bottom around the base.

"Do you like it?" he asked me, and I moaned a yes.

He climbed off the bed, and then I heard him

say from across the room, "Then you'll really like this."

The butt plug began to vibrate in my ass. I writhed against my cuffs as the pulsing moved through my body. My bare nipples ached and rubbed against the bedspread. I could tell that the crotch of my teddy was wet with pussy juice, and the vibrations pushed me closer and closer toward an orgasm. Suddenly, the vibrations stopped.

"No," I begged, "please. More."

"Not yet," he said. "We're not finished." He stood quietly across the room, not moving, not making a sound. I lay on my stomach, my face turned to the side, feeling my pussy lips tingle and ache with need. I tried to grind against the bed but the restraints held me in place. I waited and waited, feeling the near-orgasm subside. I jolted when the butt plug suddenly came to life. I moaned and screamed and nearly came, but just as the orgasm was in my grasp, Man Number Two killed the power again.

"NO!" I shouted, forcefully. "Please!"

More time passed, and tears of desperation streamed down my face. I heard Man Number Two approach the bed. He lifted my pelvis into the air a bit and thrust himself deep into my pussy—just one, long thrust. He didn't move, he didn't grind. He just filled my pussy with his cock.

"Please," I sobbed. "I need to come."

He turned on the vibrations again, this time set to a steady pulse that moved along the length of the butt plug. He didn't move, but I felt his cock pulsing, and he moaned as the vibrations grew stronger and stronger.

I couldn't hold on anymore. I squeezed down hard on his cock and the butt plug in my ass and bucked like a colt as the orgasm ripped through me. Then he came just as forcefully. Leaving the butt plug vibrating gently, he pulled himself out, and walked out of the room as I writhed with the pulsation deep in my ass.

"Are you sure you're ready for round three?" Evie asked me. I was breathing hard, but I nodded. She had pulled out the butt plug and was cleaning me with another warm, wet washcloth. She unfastened my cuffs and helped me off of the bed.

"Stand here for a moment," she said, and the door opened and closed. I knew Evie was not alone, but I didn't understand why I was standing by the bed.

"This guy has different ideas," Evie said. The

mask still covered my eyes, but I could still hear someone settling on the bed, and the now unmistakable sound of the cuffs being secured. Evie led me to the bed. "He's all yours," she said, and closed the door behind her.

I blindly reached out and felt the warm skin in front of me. I ran my fingers over the muscles in his chest, felt the pebbles of his nipples, the five o'clock shadow on his face. His cock was long and thick, velvety smooth, and pre-cum trickled from the tip.

"What do you want me to do?" I asked Man Number Three.

"Use me," he said. "Fuck me."

I started to remove the mask.

"No," Man Number Three said. "Leave the mask on."

His voice was familiar to me, but I couldn't place him. Did I know him? I felt a moment of terror at the idea of someone from my everyday life knowing my secret. I stood by the bed, unsure of what I wanted.

My tigress decided.

I climbed onto the bed, straddled his chest, and thrust my tits in his face.

"Suck on my tits," I ordered Man Number Three. He latched on to my right nipple and heat shot through me. "Oh, suck harder. Pull with your teeth." I held myself over him, relishing the pleasurable pain, squeezing and pinching my other nipple while he worked.

"God, that feels good," I said, and shifted so his mouth could latch on the left one. I caught myself grinding my crotch against his chest, and knew it was time for more. I crawled up his body, grasped the headboard with my hands, and lowered my pussy to his lips.

"Eat me," I commanded, and his tongue slipped into the open crotch of my teddy. I held myself still, barely breathing, as his tongue stroked my clit, my lips, then delved into my wet hole. He licked and sucked until my thighs started to shake and I convulsed around his face.

Gasping for air, I turned myself around. "I want to suck your cock," I told him, and he moaned. "But you can't stop eating me out," I said, positioning my pussy over his face. "If you stop, I stop."

I swirled my tongue over his head, spreading his salty pre-cum over the velvet tip and around the ridge. Man Number Three bucked his hips and pressed his tongue into my pussy.

"Good boy," I murmured, as I licked up and down the front of his shaft. I massaged his balls with my fingers and he gently sucked on my clit.

I could smell my spit mixing with the scent of his pre-cum. I licked my lips, relaxed my mouth and took his cock down my throat until my lips touched his body.

His hips jerked and he tore his mouth away from my snatch to shout. I pulled away from his cock.

Man Number Three whimpered. "Suck my clit," I said to him. "Make me come. And I'll give you the best head."

I leaned my pussy back into his face, and moaned when his tongue started stroking my clit. I took most of his cock back into my mouth, rubbing, stroking, massaging with my lips and tongue. The head oozed salty juice as his body came closer and closer to coming. His hips thrust upwards into my mouth. My own body crashed with the waves of an orgasm, and still I rode his cock with my mouth, bobbing up and down, stroking his balls. I felt the maddening ripple just before his head jerked and he came explosively in my mouth. I let it run out of my mouth as I stroked his shaft until he begged me to stop.

I felt so powerful. So sexy. So deliciously used. Before he could protest, I tore the mask away and discovered Nate, who had helped me fulfill fantasy number one. I leaned over and kissed him, loving the way his cum and my pussy juice tasted together.

My friends at work commented on the "incredibly good mood" I had been in these past few days. I felt incredible. Powerful. Yet Jake and Derek had one piece of paper left in their possession, and I was more nervous about it than either of my other two fantasies.

I'd never even seen a naked woman in person before, much less had sex with one.

Two days went by, and I wondered how much longer Jake and Derek would keep me in suspense. Then, as I put away groceries that Friday evening, I received a text message from Jake.

Bonaventure. Suite 1725. 9 p.m.

Fantasy three was going to happen.

This time, Nate answered the door. I must have looked nervous because he stroked my hair away from my face and kissed me before whispering, "You will love her," into my ear.

"Are you going to dress me tonight?" I joked.

"She doesn't want you wearing anything," he said, and led me toward a giant marble tub in the master bathroom. Lighted candles surrounded the room, and scented water filled the tub. Nate pulled the T-shirt over my head and smiled at my cornflower-blue demibra. He unbuttoned my jeans and pushed them down around my ankles.

He stroked my pussy through my cornflower-blue boy shorts. "These are pretty sexy," he said, and he kneeled in front of me to push his tongue hard against the thin fabric covering my lips. Fire pumped through my body as he stroked me with his tongue and hot breath.

"Too bad it's not my turn tonight," he said. He unhooked the bra and tossed it on the counter. He slowly pulled the boy shorts down to my ankles and helped me step out of them.

I stepped into the hot, fragrant water and gloried in Nate gently rubbing a washcloth all over my body. Then he offered me a hand out of the giant tub and dried me off.

My body hummed as Nate led me back to the bedroom.

Evie stood in front of the bed. "It's finally my turn," she murmured, and untied the single knot that held her robe in place. The silk robe fell to her feet.

I'd never unabashedly stared at a naked woman standing in front of me before. I'd never visually caressed her from her dark, shiny tresses down to her toes. I'd never really looked at another woman's tits, watched the nipples pucker, and traced the carefully maintained curls to her lips.

But I wanted to now.

"I want to watch you touch her," Nate said in my ear. Obediently, I stepped in front of Evie and looked into her blue eyes.

"I want to touch you," I said, and I stroked her face, her lips, her shoulders and arms. Evie guided my shaking hands to her tits, and for the first time in my life, I was relishing the heavy weight, the soft skin, the texture of another woman's body.

Evie moaned and leaned toward me for a kiss. There was no doubt I was kissing a woman. Her lips were so soft and gentle but no less demanding. Her tongue slipped into my mouth.

Tears burned my cheeks as I admitted to myself how wonderful it was to be kissing this woman.

She pulled away from me for a moment. "Tell me what you want, Emma," she said. I swallowed hard. Did I really want to do this? Yes, I did.

"I want to touch you," I said. "Everywhere. I want to suck on your tits. I want to feel your fingers spreading my pussy open. I want to taste your cunt. I want you to bury your face in mine." Tears streamed down my face as I realized how badly I wanted it all, and how scared I was to actually do it.

Evie stroked my face, silently reassuring me. She then looked over my shoulder to Nate, who silently moved to stand right behind me.

"I want to watch you suck on her tits, Em," he said to me. I bent in front of Evie and cupped her right breast in my hand. Her nipple puckered into a pebble, the aureole around it tight with anticipation. I latched my mouth onto her breast and stroked her nipple with my tongue. Evie arched toward me and moaned. I suckled a little harder, and Evie grabbed my shoulders as she whimpered. I stroked her other breast with my fingers as I gently grazed my teeth over the nipple in my mouth.

"The other one now," she pleaded, and I moved my mouth and attached it to her other nipple.

My own tits felt painfully heavy with the need to be touched. My nipples ached. I knew my lips were slick with pussy juice. I wondered if Evie's were, too. Without moving my mouth, I ran my hands down her sides, over her hips. Sensing what I wanted, Evie stepped her legs apart, and I stroked the insides of her thighs. My left hand moved up, up her soft skin, towards the radiant heat. I stroked the curls until my fingers found that extremely feminine slit. I traced her lips and then parted them.

My God.

So slick. So smooth. So wet. So hot.

I felt, for the first time, the nub of another woman's clit, and gently stroked it with my fingers. Over and over, I stroked the insides of her flesh, and, feeling brave, I slipped one finger deep inside her.

Evie gasped. "Bed," she panted, and stretched out on her back, her long legs bent at the knee.

I spread her legs apart with the palms of my hands and looked at her pussy. Her lips glimmered with wetness. I spread them with my fingers and watched the smooth, wet juice pool out of the very core of her. I slid two fingers inside her and marveled at the texture, the strength of her muscles.

Leaving my fingers inside, I dipped my head forward and smelled her salty, earthy scent. I felt her eyes on me as I gently licked her clit. I thought about how I liked to be handled, and stroked her clit along the sides, gently up and down, building the intensity, and then pulled away for a moment. I focused on moving my fingers in and out, in and out. Just as she started to sink back down, I wrapped my lips around her clit and sucked. I sucked and licked. Her thighs squeezed against my head. She panted, she begged. I pushed a third finger into her cunt and sucked harder.

She clenched around my fingers.

Her thighs tightened around my head.

She thrust her hips up off of the bed and into my face. I gentled my mouth on her, but didn't stop until she begged me to.

I pulled away, aware of her juice all over my face, her sweat on my skin.

I'd almost forgotten Nate was in the room until he said, "Your turn, Emma. On your back."

Evie sat up as I lay on my back. She smiled at me. "You were incredible for a first-timer," she said.

Evie straddled my hips and leaned forward so she could knead my tits. "Such a handful," she whispered, and tugged at my nipples. I bucked my hips and thrust my chest into her hands.

"You can be rough with them," I said, and cried out when she squeezed harder. She bent her head over my nipple. I couldn't take my eyes off of her as she took it into her mouth and sucked hard.

Evie held herself up on her right forearm. Her left hand stroked my stomach, down my pelvis, and moved between my thighs. My heart fluttered when her fingers dipped into my snatch, stroking, rubbing, knowing just where and how to touch.

"Hold her open for me, Nate," Evie said. Nate leaned against the bed, holding my knees apart. I could hear the wet sound of my lips being spread open by her fingers. I watched her face dip towards my cunt.

She thrust her tongue inside me. I bucked against Nate's hands.

Evie's mouth moved to my clit, her tongue stroking, licking, bringing me closer and closer to a screaming orgasm. She pushed two fingers inside me a few times, and then traced them from my pussy towards the back. Evie stroked my clit while tracing circles around my other puckered hole.

My pussy grew wetter. My asshole quivered.

Evie pushed a finger inside. I moaned.

"Yes, I know how much you like this," she said. She pushed in a second finger and roughly tongued my clit.

My asshole impaled on her fingers, my clit in her mouth, I couldn't hold on anymore. I screamed, bucking my hips, trying to close my legs, only to be held down by Nate's strong hands. My clit grew more sensitive, but Evie wouldn't let go. Instead, she pushed a third finger deep into my ass and her thumb into my pussy. Real tears of sensitive pain and pleasure poured out of my eyes.

"Hold her down, Nate," Evie said. "There is something I really want to do." She pulled her fingers out of my body and stood. She picked up a bottle of lube from the side table and flipped open the cap. Nate and I watched as she spilled lube over the fingers, palm and knuckles of her right hand.

Excitement and fear swept through me.

Nate was so hard he was going to burst out of his pants.

Evie closed her mouth over my clit again. I moaned.

She slipped one finger into my puckered hole. Then a second. Then a third.

I felt hot and tight. Juice dripped out of my pussy towards her hand. Her fingers held tightly together, Evie pulled them out for a moment and then pushed in a fourth. One knuckle in. Then two. Then the knuckles of her hand. My asshole stretched wide open as her hand moved inside, all but the thumb, which imbedded into my pussy.

I screamed, writhing, bucking, burning with pain and heat and ecstasy. I could see in my mind the erotic image of her hand holding me open. I came hard, hard, hard, squeezing her hand, her thumb, my thigh muscles aching as they fought against Nate's firm grasp.

Evie licked me gently a few more times and lifted her face. Her eyes focused on mine as she pulled her hand away. The slick, wet sound of her fingers leaving my body filled the room. I panted, stunned by the intensity, yet frustrated by how incomplete it felt.

Evie gave me a knowing smile as she headed for the bathroom.

"I think she could use some cock, Nate," she said as she closed the door.

"Do you need some cock, Emma?" Nate asked.

"I need your cock, Nate," I said. "Please."

I opened the door for Jake and Derek, who came over that morning for breakfast. Nate was in the kitchen, making French toast. Jake gleefully opened up the business journal to show me an article about my ex-boyfriend, Stephen.

I choked on my coffee as I read the headline: Exec Arrested for Fraud.

"That's just perfect," I said.

"You're looking well," Derek said, and Jake snickered into his coffee cup.

I patted Nate's hand, which was resting on my shoulder. "Life is good," I said.

And I let Nate bend me over the dining table right after Jake and Derek left.

Night Moves

By Eden Bradley

Eden Bradley is the award-winning author of numerous novels and novellas, both in print and electronic format, and her work has appeared in several erotic anthologies. Eden appears regularly on Playboy Radio and conducts workshops on the writing craft and writing about sex. A psychology major, she's fascinated with how the human mind responds to intimacy, especially when sex and romance collide. Eden lives in Hollywood. You can visit her at www.EdenBradley.com.

Kate leaned into the hard edge of the metal-framed window as the train pulled out of the station. Klamath Falls, Oregon. The least exciting town in existence. But her pulse was thrumming, anyway.

She always felt that lovely anticipation, that thrill, when she was on a train. But the biggest thrill lay ahead, after the other passengers had fallen asleep. She could hardly wait.

Her gaze caught the flash of lights on the slowly retreating platform, then there was nothing but the velvet night. Nothing to see in this part of the country. No scenery, no city lights. Didn't matter. What mattered was being there, feeling that motion, that sense of possibility, of *going*.

It was nearly midnight: far too late for the dining car. The train had been delayed, leaving her sitting in the quiet, small-town station for hours.

Good thing she'd stopped to eat as soon as she'd arrived from Ashland. Klamath Falls shut down early, and there was nothing but an old candy machine wedged between the ancient rows of wooden benches inside the station.

But that part was over now. Now there was just the luxurious idea of the long, slow ride ahead.

Something sexy about trains. She wasn't sure what it was. But she always swore she could feel that rocking motion hum through her entire body like one enormous vibrator. She was beginning to melt a little all over at the thought.

Have to be alone soon.

Thank God it was late. The lights were kept low, and most of the other passengers would be asleep soon.

She leaned back in her seat, allowed the rolling sensation to lull her, felt it pulse between her thighs.

This part was almost as good as the rest, the anticipation of her little adventures. She'd done this on trains all over the country; she never tired of it. Didn't even matter too much where she was going. *Going* was the important thing. The motion, the smooth, forward thrust of iron.

She stayed in her seat for another half hour, absorbing the hard whisper of tons of metal moving beneath her. Finally, she couldn't stay still any longer.

It's time.

She got up, hefted her overnight bag over her shoulder and moved silently down the center aisle, passing between row after row of passengers nested in for the night. But for her, the night was just beginning.

She pulled open the door, stepped onto the noisy platform between cars, opened the next door and slipped inside as quietly as she could, kept going until she reached the sleeper compartments.

She took a deep breath before opening that last door. Then she moved through, easy as water, sliding the heavy door shut behind her.

She stood in the hallway, getting her sea legs, listening, her heart a loud thrumming in her own ears. And the longer she stood there, the more the heat built between her thighs, the seam of her worn jeans rubbing there as she swayed with the motion of the train.

Soon...

The car was empty. She moved down the row, quietly trying the first doorknob. Locked. Damn.

She moved on, tried the next one. Locked. One

by one, she made her way down to the other end
of the car, slipped out with a sigh of frustration
and went on to the next car.

Just as quiet. Her head was filled with the gentle roar of the engines, the *snick* of the wheels
on the tracks. She stood a moment, savoring the
sound, the sensation, before moving on. The first
door was locked. But the second turned under the
gentle pressure of her hand.

Ah-ha!

She pulled the door back, peered into the
small, darkened compartment, her pulse ham-
mering in triumph and the flickering idea of getting caught. There was nothing on the floor or the
padded bench seat, no luggage, nothing to indi-
cate anyone was in there. She stopped anyway,
listening, but all she heard was the night rushing
by outside the window. She slipped inside, closing the door behind her.

Her skin was heating all over now, her body
humming with need. Dropping her bag onto the
bench seat, she moved to the window, leaning
her weight against the cold glass so she could
really feel the motion. She stayed there for several moments, perfectly still, absorbing it all: the
rumbling of the train, the vibration of it moving
though her body. She pressed her breasts against

the glass, the cold of the hard, sleek surface bringing her nipples up through the cotton of her T-shirt.

She was wet already. Had been for the last half hour.

With a quiet sigh, she unzipped her jeans, slipped one hand down between her thighs, beneath the lace of her panties.

Oh, yes.

She brushed at her mound, but the ache was too strong, too insistent. Like an eager lover, she pressed on her clitoris, the nub of it hard against her palm. Leaning harder into the window, she let the motion of the train move through the back of her hand. Pleasure swam in her system, hot, insistent. And when she slid two fingers into her soaking wet slit, between the swollen folds, she gasped.

Then it was too late for any show of teasing, any restraint. She plunged her fingers in deeper, rubbed the heel of her hand hard against her clit, the train moving beneath her like some monolithic lover. Pleasure rammed into her, even as her fingers did, deep, deeper.

Yes...

She rubbed harder, her body arcing into her hand, into the side of the car. She was hot all over, melting, her legs weak. And still she worked herself mercilessly, her hand and the rocking of the train drawing her climax into her. Pleasure rose, crested, and she pressed hard onto her clit, thrust her fingers in deep, and came into her hand. Moaning, gasping, as sensation overwhelmed her.

So good, always, her secret perversion. She smiled to herself.

A quiet voice came out of the dark. "Nice. Beautiful."

"Jesus!" She yanked her hand out of her pants, nearly fell onto the vinyl-covered bench.

"I'm sorry. But you came in here while I was sleeping, and I woke up…and then I couldn't interrupt you."

Her face was burning. With embarrassment, with anger, with fear. And her heart was racing at a thousand miles an hour.

"You scared the shit out of me!" She zipped her jeans with clumsy fingers. "Look, I'm…I'm going. Okay? I'll just…disappear."

"I wish you wouldn't." The voice was calm, soothing. "I'm going to turn on the light. Don't be scared, okay?"

Kate grabbed her big bag, was backing up to the door.

"I'm going to go. You...you don't need to tell anyone I was here, all right?"

God, what if this guy was some sort of pervert? But what was she, then?

The light flicked on; just a small amber glow lighting up the sleeping bunk. She blinked.

He was sitting on the edge of the bunk, all classic California surfer guy, his tousled, dirty blond hair sweeping the top of his shoulders, his neatly trimmed goatee a few shades darker. He was wearing a pair of wrinkled cargo pants and nothing else. And he was beautiful.

She couldn't move.

"Wow", he said.

"What?"

He smiled at her, blinking his eyes. They were pale, but there wasn't enough light for her to make out the shade. Gray? Green?

"What?" she repeated, her hand tightening on the strap of her heavy bag.

Why didn't she just get the hell out of there?

"You're pretty."

She laughed. "You sound surprised. But I'm not pretty."

"You are. And I guess I didn't expect you to be when it was dark and I was...watching you.

Except that I could see the silhouette of your hair."

She reached a self-conscious hand to her long, unruly blond curls. "What about my hair?"

"It's beautiful." His voice was deep and husky with sleep. Sexy. Or maybe it was just her body still simmering with the last threads of her orgasm. Or his beautiful face, his hard body…

"You must be blind."

"No, I saw everything."

"Shit. Look, I'm going to go."

She reached for the doorknob, pulled on it.

"I liked it."

Why did that stop her cold?

He pushed off from the bunk, the tiny train cabin too small for him to do anything but stand right behind her. She swore she could feel the heat emanating from his body, carrying his scent. Patchouli. Classic surfer scent. It made her shiver.

"Don't go," he said again. "My name's Ian."

She turned her head, looking over her shoulder at him, and he was right *there*. Too close. This wasn't the way it was supposed to go. It was all about her and the train. And he'd ruined it.

Hadn't he?

But her body was still loose and warm from her climax, and Ian was making her heat up all over again.

"Tell me your name," he said quietly. Gently.

"You're not going to report me?"

"I'd be an idiot if I did."

He was grinning at her now, but even though his eyes glittering in the half dark were all heat, there was nothing leering in his gaze.

She smiled back at him. "So, have you always been a voyeur?"

"Not until tonight. Have you always been an exhibitionist?"

"Yes. Always."

"I think I've just discovered that I like that in a girl."

They stood for a moment, silent, smiling, while desire hummed in the air between them like piano wire strung tight, sending out one long, lovely note.

I want you.

Oh, yes, she wanted him. Wanted him, and wanted it to be on the train. Too perfect. Too strange.

She wasn't usually one for casual sex. Not that it had never happened. She'd met a few guys in her travels. But it had only been five months since she'd broken things off with Dominic, and she'd sworn off men since then.

Now might be a good time to break her vow.

"So, you're staying?"

"I'm thinking about it," she admitted.

I must be losing my mind.

"Tell me your name," he asked her again.

"Kate."

"Kate. Nice." He put a hand on her bag. "Why don't you put this down?"

She nodded, let him take the heavy bag from her and set it on the bench. Watched as he straightened up. He wasn't quite six feet tall, maybe five foot ten, five-eleven, but since she was five four, it didn't matter. She didn't like a guy to be too tall. And he had one of those surfer bodies, all long, lean muscle, heavier around the chest and shoulders. On his left forearm was a tattoo. She reached out, ran one fingertip over the design.

"What's this?"

"A motherboard. I'm a computer tech."

"Really?"

"Really. Why? What did you expect?"

"Hmm, I'm not sure. You look a lot like one of

the guys who works at this little coffee place by my house."

He took a step closer. "And do you like the guy at your coffee place?"

"Sure." She could smell him again, could almost feel his tan skin beneath her hands. She flexed her fingers. "But not as much as I think I could like you."

"Really? How much is that?"

"Enough that I'm not running out of here the way I should."

"Yeah, this is kinda crazy. Meeting like this."

"It is."

Insane, really, that she wasn't running out the door. But she wasn't the kind of girl who played it safe. That had been one of Dominic's complaints: she was too spontaneous, he couldn't ever pin her down. Not that she wanted anyone to do that. But this…this was a little extreme, even for her. Which made being here with Ian all the more appealing.

"Kate…" he stopped, shook his head.

"What?"

"I really want to kiss you."

He was looking right at her, his gaze steady. His eyes were green, she was almost positive now. Beautiful against his tanned skin.

"I really want you to."

"You don't know me."

"It doesn't matter. I don't know why, but it doesn't. There's even sort of something…great about that. Mysterious. Do you know what I mean?"

"Yeah, I do."

"So, are you going to kiss me, Ian?"

"Yeah, I am."

He lowered his head. Yes, she must have lost her mind, to be here with this stranger. But she didn't want to think about that now. No, all she wanted to think about was how lush his mouth was up close, how good his skin smelled. She reached up, slid her hand around the back of his neck, under his long hair, and pulled him down to her.

His lips met hers, soft at first. So soft. She went warm all over, just heating up like crazy even before he slid his tongue into her mouth. And then there was nothing soft about what was happening between them. It was all need, hunger. He pressed his mouth to hers, hard, bruising, but it was exactly what she needed. Even better when he slid his arm around her and pulled her in close, until she could feel his erection through the fabric of his clothes and hers.

His mouth was so sweet. The guy could kiss, that was for damn sure. Her breath was just going out of her body.

He pulled back, whispered, "Damn, girl. I need to touch you. Okay?"

"Yes. Please."

He pulled her T-shirt over her head, then stood and stared. "Perfect," he whispered. Reaching out, he stroked her stomach with one finger, making her pulse flutter, sending heat like warm, wet lightning to her sex. Sharp. Electric. And the train rumbling beneath them, carrying them through the night, a heavy undercurrent of tension, of pure sex.

"Come on, Ian," she pleaded.

"Come on, what?"

"Let's get naked. It's too good to wait."

He nodded, his face tight with need. He slipped one of her bra straps down, then the other, before stepping back in close to her. Reaching behind her, he rested his head on her shoulder, his goatee a little rough against her skin as he unsnapped her bra. It fell away, and he pressed closer, bare skin to bare skin.

"Yes, just like that," she breathed.

He pressed harder, crushing her breasts against the solid wall of his chest, moving her body until her back was up against the cool metal of the door. He was kissing her again, his mouth on hers, his tongue slipping between her lips, thrusting into her mouth in some primal rhythm, his hips grinding into hers in the same tempo. And the hushed roar of the train like music. Like sex itself.

She groaned. Let her hands wander, smoothing over his skin, feeling the rise and curve of muscle in his shoulders, his back. Even the sensation of his skin under her hands was erotic to her.

He moved back then, just an inch or two, enough to get his hands in between them, to cup her breasts, teasing her nipples immediately with his thumbs into two hard, aching points.

"Ah, you like that."

"Yes."

He took her nipples between his thumbs and his forefingers, pinched a little, drew them out.

"And that?"

"Yes. Oh…"

"You're so hot, Kate," he said, his voice low, nearly a whisper. "Your skin, your breasts, your mouth." He squeezed her nipples, hard, and she moaned softly. "So hot. So responsive. I can barely stand it. I'm so damn hard. Feel me, Kate."

He pushed against her, the hard ridge of his cock pressing into her belly.

"Ian...come on."

"Yeah..."

He worked quickly, slipping out of his cargo shorts, then a pair of dark boxers. His cock was fully erect, thick. Beautiful. She felt her mouth water. Felt her pussy go tight.

Need it. Need him. Yes...

And the fact that this was happening here, on the train. Like every fantasy she'd ever had, all of those nights getting herself off while a train going somewhere, anywhere, moved beneath her. Drove her. Made her come as much as her hand moving frantically between her thighs.

Ian went down on his knees, slipping her jeans off, then her panties. Still on his knees before her, just breathing on the narrow strip of hair between her thighs. Warm. Excruciating, to make her wait.

She buried her fingers in his hair, pulled a little, spread her thighs, inviting him. And gasped when he planted a single, small kiss there.

"Don't tease me, Ian. I can't take it right now."

"Yes, you can. I'm going to enjoy this."

"Fuck, Ian."

"Yeah, we'll get to that. But you're too good to rush through."

She groaned, forcing herself to still while he used his fingers to hold her pussy lips apart. While he held her open like that and just breathed on her.

God...

She waited, her juices trickling down the inside of one thigh. The sight of his beautiful body bent before her, his silky blond hair tickling her skin, was almost too much for her. That and the lovely, smooth motion of the wheels against the tracks.

Finally, he moved his fingers, massaging her nether lips. Slowly, slowly, working one finger toward her waiting hole, and then, dipping inside.

"Oh!"

"Yeah, girl. It's good, isn't it?" he murmured. "I want to see you squirm before I make you come."

"Yes, Ian..."

He leaned in, and she could feel his warm breath on her again, before he flicked his tongue at her clit.

She arced her hips.

He did it again, and again, his tongue like some tiny, wet lance, driving pleasure deep into her body. And his fingers still holding her apart, one buried deeper inside her.

Her legs were shaking, need like some sort of drug coursing through her veins. And when he took her clit into his hot, wet mouth and sucked, she exploded.

Pleasure shafted into her, deep, deeper, leaving her shuddering.

"Fuck, Ian!"

He worked her hard with his fingers, his mouth, until she was breathless, spent. Then he pulled away.

"Oh, yeah, I'm going to fuck you."

Before the last waves of her climax had faded, he had her on the edge of the small bunk.

"Wait here."

He fumbled in a backpack on the bed, pulled out a small foil pouch, and she watched as he sheathed himself.

"Spread for me, beautiful girl. Yeah, that's it."

Her thighs fell open wide, and as he stood before her, she reached for him, pulling his hips into hers. He stopped at the entrance to her sex. She could feel the tip against her wet opening.

"Come on, Ian. Come on and fuck me."

He let out a long breath. Slid in an inch. Pleasure pulsed in her blood, in her sex.

"Deeper."

Another inch, and his cock was already beginning to fill her up. She surged against him.

"You want it all?"

"Oh, yes."

He reached out a hand, caught her hair up in his fingers, twined them there, pulling tight, and plunged deep, burying himself inside her.

"Oh!"

"Jesus, you feel good," he murmured, before he began to move.

Her fingers dug into the flesh of his hips as he drove into her, over and over, pleasure burrowing into her with every sharp thrust. Her legs were wrapped around his narrow waist, holding him tight against her. And when she looked up at him, his face, drawn in ecstasy, was one of the most beautiful things she'd ever seen.

"I just need to fuck you, Kate. Just fuck you."

"Yes, do it. Do it hard."

He slammed into her, the wool blanket on the bunk scratching her skin, the metal frame below the thin mattress biting into her spine. She didn't care. All she knew was she had never felt so taken over, never been fucked so hard in her life. Never been fucked to the rhythm of the train that was pure sex to her. And she loved every minute of it.

She rocked against him, rocked with the turning of heavy iron wheels over solid iron tracks. Something so primal, so basic. And the scent of sex was all around her. The scent of sex, of Ian's skin, of her own juices.

"Fuck me harder, Ian. Come on, you can do it."

He drove into her, pummeling her, his pubic bone crashing into hers, and she was coming again, panting, her pussy clenching in pleasure. It spread, deep into her body, into her mind, while a thousand stars went off in her head. Blinding. Beautiful.

He was still fucking her, his body going hard all over. Then he tensed, shuddered, muttered, "Jesus, girl, have to fuck you, fuck you, yeah…"

The train kept moving, sliding over the rails, while they breathed together, the air pungent with their sweat, with the tangy scent of sex, the earthier scent of come as he pulled the condom off.

He pulled her with him onto the narrow bunk while they caught their breath. His body was warm, felt good against hers. One arm was looped beneath her shoulder, and he idly played with her hair.

"That was perfect," she told him.

"Yeah it was."

"Ian…"

"Hmm?"

"I want to tell you something. It's easier because I don't know you."

He laughed softly, a deep chuckle. "You know me now, girl."

"Maybe. But I still want to tell you."

"Okay."

"I have a…fetish. It's about the trains."

"Ah, so that's what it was all about earlier, you making yourself come like that."

"Yes. I've done it before. As often as I can. I love to ride the train, but even more, I love to wait until it's night, then find an unlocked compartment, and bring myself off."

He was quiet a moment, then, "And? Is that all?"

"Yes. No. Part of it is sneaking in here like this, you know? Doing something I'm not supposed to do. It's fucking thrilling as hell, if you want to know the truth. I've done it a few times now. And it gets better every time. It starts sooner each time. I was wet the moment I got on the train tonight. I had to find a place to be alone, had to get myself off."

He groaned. "I'm getting hard again just hearing you tell me these things. But that's not the only reason why I'm glad you told me."

They were both quiet for a while. Then she said, "This is…almost magical for me. Like something I made up."

"Maybe you did."

"Maybe. But you're real. You're experiencing this, too. My fantasy."

"Yeah. But it's mine, too. Meeting a beautiful girl on the train in the middle of the night. How often does that happen to anyone?"

"I'm not beautiful."

"It's true. I don't know why you don't think so."

"I'm too skinny and my hair is totally out of control."

"That's what I like about it. It's wild. Like you. And your skin is like fucking silk. Like pale silk."

"You don't have to say that."

"Yeah, and you didn't have to stay here. Didn't have to sleep with me. But you did."

"Because I wanted to."

"That's right."

She was quiet a moment. "Okay."

She smiled to herself, and he pulled her chin up, kissed her, his tongue slipping between her lips. She was hot all over again immediately.

"Kiss me like that and I'll believe anything you say," she told him when he pulled away. "I'll do anything you say."

"That's very tempting."

"I mean it."

And she did. Maybe it was the train. Maybe it was something about him. She didn't even know him. But it didn't matter. All that mattered was how much she wanted him, craved his touch. His mouth, his hands on her flesh.

"Why do you trust me so much?" he asked her.

"I don't know. But I do."

"You don't know anything about me."

"Sure I do. I know you're a tech geek."

He laughed. "Yeah. Do you want to know more? Or do you want to just be strangers who fucked on a train?" There was nothing bitter in his question. He was simply asking her.

"Yes. I want to know more." She did, she realized. "Tell me where you're from. Are you going home?"

"Yeah, heading home from Bend, to Huntington Beach."

"Ah, do you surf?"

"Everyone in Huntington surfs."

"And what were you doing in a nowhere town like Bend, Oregon?"

"I went to my uncle's funeral."

"Shit. I'm sorry."

"No, it's okay. I never liked him much. I went because I thought I should. Because my family expected it."

"Do you always do what other people expect of you?"

"Almost never. But this time…I don't know. I knew it'd make my mother happy. And no, I'm not a mama's boy."

"I don't think mama's boys can fuck like that."

He laughed. "So, what about you? Where are you off to? Did you get on in Klamath Falls, or were you already on the train?"

"Yes, I got on in Klamath. I was in Ashland for a week with some friends at the Shakespeare Festival. Have you ever been?"

"No. But I've heard about it."

"It's a pretty amazing thing, if you like theater. Do you?"

"Yeah, I do. I um…I played Puck in my high school production of *A Midsummer Night's Dream*."

"Really?"

"Yeah, really."

"I like that. A guy who knows Shakespeare."

"We're not all football-playing jarheads."

"Maybe not all of you."

He grinned at her, smoothed her hair from her face.

"So, where's home? And what do you do there besides read Shakespeare?"

"San Francisco. I'm a graphic artist. I work freelance. It lets me travel."

"I love San Francisco. Love the food there. And they have some of the best beer bars."

"Have you ever been to Zeitgeist?"

"Yeah, that biker bar? The best ale anywhere."

She nodded. "I love living in San Francisco. I have a place down by the ocean. I love the fog, the loneliness of it. The grayness." She stopped, laughed. "You probably think that's strange."

"No, not at all. I like to go out surfing in the morning, and I mean really early. Five, six a.m. It's always foggy that early. Peaceful. Like it's just me and the ocean out there. And the ocean is endless and powerful. It wipes everything else away. Whatever is on my mind. Job stress, whatever. I take my dog with me, and he just sits on the sand and watches me."

"I like dogs. What's his name?"

"Petey. Do you know the dog in that old show, *The Little Rascals*? He's a pit bull and he looks just like that—white with a black ring around one eye."

"Yes, of course I know that show. I love old black-and-white television. All those shows from the fifties and sixties. *I Love Lucy*. *The Honeymooners*. Everything was so simple. These days, everyone wants everything at once."

He was watching her again, his pale eyes all dark pupil now, glittering. "All I want right now is to kiss you. To make you come again."

She smiled as he rolled her onto her back, laid his long body on top of hers. Straddling her, he bent so he didn't hit his head on the top bunk. He started by running his hands over her skin: her stomach, her throat, her shoulders, making her nipples peak hard, wanting to be touched.

"Come in, Ian," she said quietly.

He laughed. "You're impatient, girl."

"I am. You said you'd make me come."

"Oh, I will."

He took both nipples in his fingers and pinched hard, making her gasp.

"Good?" His eyes were gleaming in the half dark.

"Oh, yes."

He pushed her breasts together, leaned in and traced his tongue over one hard tip. She moaned, pleasure filling her up, spreading into her arms, her legs, her sex.

"Oh, I like that. Don't stop." It came out a quiet, breathless whisper.

He paused, looked up at her, his lush mouth crooked in a half smile. "I won't. Not since you asked so nicely." He bent his head once more, his hair falling onto her chest, stroking her skin as his tongue went back to work, lapping, licking.

He went from one nipple to the other, his hands hot on her skin, his tongue wet, unbelievable. Desire ran like a current through her body, lighting up her sex with need. She arced her hips, but he stayed focused on her breasts, his tongue like some lovely sort of torture.

"God, Ian."

He pulled one nipple into his mouth, just letting it rest against the softness of his tongue, not moving.

"Ian. I need…I need more."

But he held still, the wet texture of his mouth on her making her crazy with need, lust pulsing between her thighs, aching.

"Ian…suck, please."

He took the hard nub between his teeth, grazing the surface, and even that brought a sharp twinge of pleasure. He moved to the other breast, took her nipple between his teeth, this time biting into the flesh a little.

"Oh, yes…"

Then he went still again. She was panting, her breath coming in short, sharp gasps. She couldn't believe what he was doing to her. Her pussy was drenched, hurting, hungry. She almost felt as though she could come like this: just his hands, his mouth, on her breasts.

Her hips arced, and she wanted to squeeze her thighs together, but Ian's body was in between them. If only he'd shift the tiniest bit, just press on her mound with one strong thigh. With his hard, lovely cock.

He lifted his head. "Patience, Kate." He laughed a little, a husky sound low in his throat. "I've got you. Don't worry."

She groaned as he squeezed both nipples in his fingers.

"You like that."

"Yes!"

He was watching her, his gaze on hers as he squeezed again.

"Oh!"

"So beautiful…"

He kept twisting, tugging, pulling on the pink flesh, and she felt her nipples swell impossibly.

Her sex pulsed, hot and wet. And his face over her, his teeth coming down on his lush lower lip, concentrated lust making his features soft.

Too good...

She was going to come.

"Yeah, that's it. I can feel it, girl. Your body going tight. I bet if I slipped my hand between your thighs your pussy would be so damn wet, I could slide right in. Like silk."

"Yes...please, Ian."

"But I'm not going to do it. I'm going to make you come, just like this. I know you can do it."

"Yes...oh, God..."

He twisted again, pain and pleasure mingling in some unfathomable way, making her shiver, making her sex clench. So close...

"Come on, girl, you can do it. Come for me."

He tugged hard, her nipples stinging in pain. But the pleasure was so intense, surging into her body, shafting deep inside her sex, like his cock, like his fingers inside her, like his mouth sucking, sucking. Except it was only his clever hands, every sensation carrying from her tortured nipples, screaming through her system, until...

"Oh! Fuck, Ian!"

Her climax ripped through her, shuddering,

explosive. And she shook all over with it, hardly believing it was happening in some dark corner of her mind. Then she was just melting, her muscles going lax, pleasure still humming through her like the thundering motion of the train beneath them.

She squeezed her eyes shut, fought to catch her breath.

"That was good," he murmured. "So damn good, just watching your face. Fucking beautiful."

He let her lay there for a few minutes, quiet. Then he lifted her chin. "Hey, girl."

"Hmm, what?" She let her eyes flutter open.

"I need to fuck you. Now."

Before she could answer he was lifting her, his hands circling her waist. He pulled her upright, off the bunk and onto her feet, pushed her up against the window so she could see the velvet sky racing by, a sliver of moon shining through the clouds. He was right up against her, his warm body pressed against her spine. Using his thigh, he made her spread her legs, pulled her hips back toward his until she felt the swollen head of his cock against her buttocks, then between her thighs.

She was still drenched from her orgasm, but

the lips of her sex were swelling with need already.

"Yes, do it, Ian."

"I will, girl."

She heard the small, metallic rip of a condom packet, waited while he pulled away to sheath himself. Then his big body was up against her once more, and he slid into her, hard and sleek, filling her.

God, she needed this. Needed it rough and hard, with no time to catch her breath as he began to pump into her right away. He used his body to press her up against the side of the train, her bare breasts on the icy glass of the window. It felt good on her sore nipples. It all felt good. Unbelievable.

"You love the feel of the train, don't you? The vibration."

"Yes…" Even hearing him say it sent a shiver of pleasure through her, beating hot and urgent in her thready pulse.

He slipped one hand around her waist, dipped down until the heel of his hand was flat against her mound. He found her clit, pressed there.

"Yes, just like that."

He pushed her with his hips, until her body was hard against the side of the train, the metal wall pressing against the back of his hand. And that vibration carried through his hand to her clit, like the enormous vibrator she'd imagined earlier. Only so much better this time, with his cock thrusting in and out of her.

"Ah, Ian, it's almost too much," she panted.

"You can take it, girl."

His voice was rough with pleasure, and she loved hearing it; loved to hear him on that brink, where control was so easily lost. Lovely. Intense.

"Fuck me harder, Ian."

"Yeah…"

He drove into her, his cock shafting deep, pushing pleasure through her sex and deep into her body, like something heavy and liquid. Pleasure like lava, flowing, spreading. In moments she was coming again, falling over that lovely, keen edge, pleasure a dazzling flash of light. Blinding. Stark.

He tensed, rammed harder into her, called out, even as she shook with her own climax still. He was holding her so tightly, his fingers digging into her skin. Didn't matter. Nothing mattered but his cock inside her, his hand, the rocking of the train.

Iron and come and flesh.

Her legs were weak, and his thighs trembled

behind her. But he held her up. As her eyes refocused, she saw a moonlit field flash by in a dark watercolor stream, the silhouette of mountains in the distance. Beautiful.

His body was so warm against hers. And the train seemed almost like a living beast, like some creature that was part of the sex, or maybe some driving force behind it. She couldn't seem to separate it all, somehow. Not now; she was too dazed.

"Come on, Kate."

He took her with him as he rolled onto the bunk, held her against his side. He was all heat and smooth, bare skin. He smelled like sex.

She curled into his heat, his half-hard cock pressed against the small of her back. He felt good. She was relaxed, loose. More comfortable than she'd been in a long time.

She'd never been this comfortable with Dominic. Never been so unself-conscious, so much *herself* with him. Maybe it was something about not really knowing Ian? About understanding that she'd get off this train and never see him again.

It seemed important to her suddenly, being who she was, finally. Maybe the universe had conspired to put her here with Ian for this purpose? Or was she being melodramatic, reading more into the situation than was really there?

But she was too tired to think about it. She inhaled deeply, pulling in the scent of Ian's skin, that dark patchouli, along with the distant scent of the countryside rushing past the windows. Soon, she slept.

Early sunlight behind her closed eyelids, invading her easy sleep. She stretched, felt the solid weight and heat of Ian's body still lying beside her.

Nice.

His voice was rough with too little sleep. "Hey, morning, girl." He ran a hand through her tangled hair, tugging on it.

Smiling, she turned to him. "Hey."

He kissed her then, a light brush of lips against hers, his goatee soft on her skin. Sweet. Romantic.

Don't start thinking this is a romance.

No, but whatever it was, it was lovely.

"Kate, we'll be at the Oakland station in a little over an hour. That's where you get off, right?"

"Oh." She looked at her watch. "Yes."

He raised himself on one arm, looked down at her, and she saw for the first time the pure, pale green of his eyes, like a calm summertime sea. His face was too serious, making her heart pound.

"We don't have much time," he said.

She swallowed. She didn't want it to matter so much.

Pulling him to her, she kissed him hard. In moments he was on top of her, grinding his hips against hers, and they panted together, breathed each other in. He found another condom in his backpack. And then he didn't stop kissing her, even as he drove into her body, as she wrapped her legs around his waist, pulling him deeper into her.

The sex was hard and fast. Desperate. Was she the only one feeling like this? But he thrust harder, fucking her, fucking her, fucking all thought from her mind. And pleasure was like the train itself, like moving iron pounding through her system; that heavy, that powerful.

When she came this time she just broke, shattered, her body shaking hard all over. And the train rumbling away on its tracks, the churning motion of the wheels, blurred, dimmed, until there was only Ian, his cock, what he was making her feel.

Soon he tensed, shivered as he came into her

body, his mouth still hard on hers. Wet, demanding, pulling pleasure from her even as her climax faded away.

He took her with him as he rolled off her, pulling her body on top of his in the narrow bunk.

"Jesus, Kate. Jesus, girl."

"Yeah."

He looked up at her, his eyes glassy with pleasure, his lush mouth slack, his lips swollen. His dirty blond hair was wild. She wanted to kiss him all day, wanted to just eat him up. Wanted to remember him exactly like this.

"You are so damn beautiful," she whispered to him.

He smiled at her. Dazzling. When he reached up and stroked a lock of hair from her face, his fingertips lingering to brush her cheek, her heart thudded in her chest.

No, don't do this....

She looked away. "Are you hungry? I'm starving."

"Yeah, I could eat. Uh, I think the dining car opens at six."

She nodded, got up and found her clothes, fumbled her way into them.

He got dressed, and they stopped to use the restrooms before wandering down the long aisles until they reached the dining car. It had just opened, and there were only a few other people there. He insisted on buying breakfast: coffee and blueberry muffins. They sat at a table, the morning light making her feel raw, vulnerable, highlighting the hair on his arms, his goatee, his eyelashes, in gold and red.

"Hey, what's up with you this morning?" he asked her. "Do you regret last night? Do you regret meeting me?"

"What? No. Of course not."

"What is it then? You've been so…wide open with me. And now you're all closed up."

"Shit. I'm sorry. I'm just…you know, I was thinking at some point in the night how easy I feel with you. And I liked it. I don't feel like I have to pretend to be anything I'm not. But this morning…"

"What is it?"

What was there to say but the truth? There was no point in doing anything else, not with Ian.

She shrugged. "I'm getting off the train in Oakland and taking BART back to San Francisco. And you're going on to Huntington. Going home."

"Yeah."

"I mean, your dog is waiting for you. Your life."

He nodded his head.

"I just wish…"

"Yeah. Me, too."

He reached out, took her hand across the table. "But do you regret it, Kate?"

"No. I don't."

It was true.

"Look, we don't live that far apart," he said. "I could make the drive in six hours."

"That long-distance stuff, it's so hard."

"It's not impossible."

"I don't know. Maybe it is. Everyone has this dreamlike expectation of what things will be like, but then stuff comes up and someone always ends up disappointed. It's silly for us to make each other any promises after one night. You can't base anything on that."

"Maybe."

"Ian, I really like you. I love what's happened between us. And I don't want to fuck that up. This has been…beautiful, if you want to know the truth. Maybe we should just leave it that way."

He was quiet a moment, his eyes going dark. Then, "Yeah, okay. Whatever you want, Kate."

He looked too damn serious. Then he reached out, stroked her cheek with one fingertip, smiled at her, those dazzling white teeth, and everything seemed okay again. Everything seemed right.

"Come on—we'd better go get your bag. We're almost there."

She let him lead her back through the train, the sound of the wheels on the tracks seeming too loud in her ears, the morning light too bright, making her wince.

They reached his compartment, and the conductor announced her stop over the loudspeaker.

Ian grabbed her hand. "Let me help you off."

She shook her head, the train screeching a little as it pulled into the station. She could see it from the corner of her eye through the window, could see the cold concrete of the city in the distance.

"I'm just going to go. Okay?"

He paused, his eyes locking on hers. She waited, thinking he was going to say something, but he just shook his head. "Yeah, okay."

She squeezed his hand tight. Then he pulled her into his arms, kissed her, his mouth coming down hard on hers, his coffee-scented lips, his tongue, so damn sweet. She let herself melt into him because that was exactly what she wanted to do.

Be myself.

He let her go, took a step back. "Better get going."

He smiled at her, and she nodded, heaved her bag onto her shoulder, turned and walked through the door.

"Fuck, fuck, fuck," she muttered under her breath as she made her way to the next car, went down the stairs, stepped onto the quiet platform. All around her the city was gray, bleak. Lonely. But she couldn't move, couldn't go until the damn train pulled away.

She waited while a handful of new passengers boarded, waited while the train idled, then lurched forward, iron wheels grating on iron tracks. Frantic suddenly, she tried to find the window of Ian's compartment, but the windows all looked the same.

"Fuck."

She hadn't even gotten his last name, his phone number, e-mail.

She ran a hand through the wild tangle of her hair, pulled tight.

If she was really going to be herself, be true to herself, she would have stayed on the train, asked Ian if she could go to L.A. with him, spend some time with him, get to know him. Take that chance. Wasn't part of being yourself living without regrets?

The train was gaining speed, wind rushing past her, pushing her hair into her eyes. She wiped it away, her vision clearing as the last of the train left the station.

Ian stood on the other side of the tracks.

He was smiling, looking a little unsure. She grinned back, her heart pounding a lovely rhythm in her body. And his smile broke, lighting up his face. Dazzling. Brilliant.

Without taking his eyes off her, he stepped onto the tracks, crossed over and took her in his arms.

Going Down

By Saskia Walker

Saskia Walker says: I'm British by birth, but because of my parents' nomadic tendencies I grew up traveling the globe – an only child with a serious book habit. I dreamed of being a writer since the age of 12 and finally began writing seriously in the late 1990s. By then I'd got myself a BA in Art and Cultural History, a Masters in Literature and the Visual Arts – and I'd worked in all manner of diverse careers – but the stories in my head simply had to be written! I was first published in the small press under the guidance of the British fantasy writer, Storm Constantine. As well as fantasy and romance, I was also dabbling in erotica. I wanted to incorporate all these elements in my writing and more. My first erotic short story was published by Virgin publishing's Black Lace imprint in 1997. From then on every spare moment was spent on the stories that bubbled away in my imagination. Nowadays I live in the north of England – close to the beautiful, windswept landscape of the Yorkshire moors – with my real life hero, Mark. Mark supports my work through all its ups and downs, and runs the tech side of this website. He also manages to keep me sane and grounded when fiction threatens to take over.

"Just as well I like a good challenge," I murmured to myself as I assessed the antique elevator shaft in my new abode. The ostentatious wrought-iron affair was the most complicated contraption I'd ever seen.

When I'd arrived at the apartment block the evening before I'd used the stairs, allowing the concierge to take my luggage in the elevator. I wanted to get my bearings, and as I climbed the stairs to the fourth floor I took in the elegance of the beautiful building, a nineteenth century block in the 15th Arrondissement of Paris. I'd been allocated a small apartment there for my six-month stint working in the city.

The elevator ran up the center of the building. The much more solid looking marble staircase wound around it, and I'd peered in at the elevator shaft as I worked my way up to the fourth floor. Although daunting, it was a beautiful thing, all black metal and designed in the Art Nouveau style. The frenzy of decorative metalwork did not distract me from the fact that the floor appeared to be scarcely more than a metal grid and one could see the cables and the whole shaft from inside and out.

This morning I had my smartest outfit and heels on and I figured I'd better try it out. The question was how to operate it. I leaned in to the metal gates and peered down the shaft. The elevator was stationary, two floors below.

"Going down?"

I jolted upright, startled to find I was no longer alone.

Turning on my heels I faced the man who had spoken.

I don't know what surprised me the most, that he had approached me without me realizing, or that he knew I was English and had spoken to me in my own language. He was obviously French.

French and gorgeous.

Dressed entirely in black—open-neck shirt and jeans, with a tailored leather jacket—he observed me with blue eyes that contrasted starkly with his swarthy skin. His black hair was cropped close, the square line of his jaw, angled cheekbones and strong forehead giving him a distinctive look. Even though I wore my highest heels, he towered over me. He had to be a neighbor. Perhaps he'd been on his way down the stairs when he'd caught sight of me. I straightened my skirt, aware that I'd probably just given him an eyeful as I peered down the shaft.

He gestured at the elevator gates. "It bothers you, the cage?"

The cage. What an intriguing moniker, and so appropriate. "Not at all," I fibbed. "I think it's beautiful, I just wasn't quite sure how to operate it."

"Allow me to demonstrate."

He rested his hand against my back briefly, encouraging me. The momentary contact made me sizzle. He pressed the call button. It was round, ivory and encased in gleaming brass. The elevator cable tightened with a loud creak then the mechanism *whirred* into action and the cage loomed up from below.

"Some of the tenants in this building won't use it, but it is quite safe and an object of some beauty." The seductive allure in his voice had my attention well and truly hooked.

"Absolutely, it's a work of art in itself."

There was an approving expression in his eyes.

Once the elevator shunted into position, he unlatched the gates, internal and external, and rolled them apart. I stepped into the cage, as he called it, and he closed the gates behind us. The shunting of metal and wheels, and the resolute sound of the internal latch did make it feel cagelike, and yet light shone through here and there beneath our feet. He pressed the button for the ground floor and the elevator jolted into action. Adrenaline pumped through my veins and I staggered slightly on my heels.

My companion turned to face me and his mouth moved in sensual appreciation as his gaze made a slow circuit of my body. I felt stripped to the bone. I'd never felt such intense scrutiny. It wasn't staring exactly. It was as if he could gain the measure of me by looking at me that way. He stood with one hand around a decorative metal coil, the other rested on his hip. His posture was so self-assured, appearing languid but as if he could pounce at any moment. What was more unnerving, the way he made me feel, or the fact I could see the elevator shaft between the metal fretwork beneath my feet? As we descended I felt as if I was on a dangerous precipice, in every way.

When his gaze returned to meet mine, his

mouth lifted at the corners. Had I met with his approval? Moving my laptop case from one hand to the other, I tried not to feel quite so self-aware. It was hard not to, and my out-fit—which had seemed businesslike and pro-fessional—now seemed far too tight-fitting and alluring. It was the way he admired the curve of my body at breast and hips that made me feel that way. Almost as if I'd been touched. What would it be like, I wondered, to really be touched by him? The man exuded sex appeal. Get a grip, I told myself, embarrassed. I'd only been with the man a few seconds, and now my face was growing hot and I was in danger of making a fool of myself. The liberation of being in a strange, exciting city, perhaps. Or maybe it was all down to my com-panion.

"Is it the original elevator?" I asked, in an effort to break the tension I felt building inside me.

"Yes, it was built in 1899. Apparently it was almost ripped out in the 1970s. There was talk of replacing it with a modern box, but luckily it did not go ahead. It would have been a tragedy to lose it."

A man who appreciated the fine things in life. I wondered what else there was to discover about my charming neighbor. Despite the fact I worked with diplomats and government officials, it was rare that I met someone quite so intriguing.

When the elevator came to a halt on the ground floor, he put his hand on the latch but paused. He was close to me, dangerously close. I could smell his cologne, sharp and musky, and it invaded my senses, making me ache for contact.

"You live underneath me," he stated.

Underneath him. Why did that made me think of sex? Because he was so damn sexy.

"If I play my music too loud," he continued, "you must please inform me." He opened the gates.

I recalled hearing the faint strains of classical music the night before as I fell asleep, but it hadn't bothered me—quite the contrary. So, it had come from his apartment. "I liked what I heard last night," I responded as I stepped out into the reception area.

"I'm glad to hear it. I'm a producer. I work in a studio in the daytime but sometimes I bring samples home to listen to in a different environment." He closed the gates securely behind us. "The gates must be closed properly, or it will not be able to collect anyone else who calls it."

We walked across the checkerboard-tiled hallway together, heading for the glass entrance doors.

"So, will you choose to enter *La Cage* again?"

A smile hovered around his handsome mouth, and his eyes glinted. That sounded like a loaded question. He knew how it came across, I was sure of it. Anticipation built at my center, my blood rushing in my veins. "Oh, yes, I enjoyed the ride immensely. Thank you."

I met his gaze, my smile lingering. I wanted him to know I was interested. I was single and in Paris, of course I'd thought about the possibility of meeting new people. Mostly I thought the opportunity would come my way through my job.

As we left the building the concierge saluted us from his reception post, a polished oak and glass office at one side of the hallway.

"May I offer you a drive to your workplace?" My companion nodded at a sleek black Mercedes parked on the opposite side of the street.

"Thank you, but a colleague is meeting me at the Metro station." Would I have accepted if I'd been able to? Of course I would. Looking up into his sharp blue eyes I wondered what that sensuous mouth would feel like covering mine, and I couldn't deny it.

"*Au revoir*, Jennifer."

My breath caught. Warning signals sounded in my mind. "How did you know my name?"

"I am your landlord, as well as your neighbor." He offered his hand. "Armand Lazare."

The strength of his handshake made me feel as if it was holding me up. Or maybe it was because my legs turned weak under me when he touched me. Then he took my hand to his lips, and kissed the back of it. When he released me, I had to reach out for the marble pillar at the bottom of the steps to steady myself. My stay in Paris had launched in the most delectable way.

"*Au revoir*," I whispered as I watched him dart across the road toward his car. I couldn't help admiring the view. His tall frame was limber and fit, broad at the shoulder and narrow at the hips. Gathering myself as quickly as I could, I headed off towards the Metro station before he could look back and see my gawking..

The encounter kept flitting through my mind over the course of that day, my moments in *La Cage* with my upstairs neighbor haunting me in the most intimate way—keeping me simmering and alert.

That night as I lay in my bed listening to the faint strains of his music, I stroked my body to a delicious peak as I thought about him. The underlying rock beat to the classical score seemed to get under my skin, fueling my lascivious thoughts. I saw myself in the cage, back to the metal struts, with his hands on me. Going down? The way he'd said that made me picture myself on my knees in *La Cage*, my hands on his belt, opening it while he stared at me with those intense eyes. When he'd spoken to me, before he let me free from the cage, he'd been so close I could smell his cologne. I wanted him closer still. I stared up at the ceiling, imagining him over me in a different way, naked and eager and thrusting.

In time to the music, I ran my fingers back and forth over my swollen clit, following the rhythm of the music, letting my fantasies run wild, letting Armand Lazare fill my senses until I found my release.

The following morning Armand ran down the steps as I locked my door.

"Good morning, Jennie."

"*Bonjour*, Armand." Was it obvious that I was grinning because we had coincided again? I didn't care.

He gestured at the elevator. "Shall we?"

As he latched the doors closed and turned to

face me I took a deep breath and savored the feeling of being alone with him in that confined space. Although he did not move, he seemed always to be prowling. It was his nature, I realized.

We began our slow descent.

"Are you enjoying your work at the embassy?"

His question leveled me, momentarily. He knew what I did. The embassy probably had to tell him who was moving into the apartment they'd rented. I imagined what they might have said—single female, conference and events organizer. Was he single? I hadn't seen him with anyone, but that didn't prove a thing.

"It's going well, thank you. I'm settling in and finding my way around. Their elevator is not as beautiful as yours, though."

I wanted to talk about him, not me. Was I being obvious?

"There aren't many quite so beautiful." He stroked one of the metal struts as he spoke, and the action did bad things to me, making the heat between my thighs build, fast.

"I heard your music last night, while I was in bed. It was beautiful."

He inclined his head, accepting the compliment gracefully. Humor lit his eyes. I felt as if he knew what I'd done while listening to that music. Why did I think that? Because I wanted him to know? Something about the man made me feel decadent and wanton. I wanted the space between us to disappear and for him to touch me.

"Do you live alone?" I asked.

"Yes." No hesitation.

I nodded. His gaze held mine. We were circling each other, the mutual interest overtly reciprocated. When the elevator jolted to halt I gasped aloud. I'd been taken unawares, my attention fixed on him as it was. He stepped over to me and steadied me with one hand beneath my elbow.

"Thank you," I whispered breathlessly.

There was some kind of commotion in the reception, a delivery.

"May I offer you a drive?" he asked, before he even broke contact with me.

Once again I had to refuse. My colleague was determined to guide me through the Metro for the rest of that week.

By Monday, however, I wanted to be able to say yes.

The following day was Friday, and as I left my apartment I figured I could ask Armand what I should do during my first weekend of free time in Paris.

Alas, there was no sign of him. I waited by my door, lingering while I put my keys into my shoulder bag. He did not appear. I checked my watch. It was a quarter to eight, exactly the same time I had left my apartment on the previous days.

I hovered expectantly by the elevator but he still didn't appear. Then I noticed that the elevator was there on my floor, as if it had been left there specifically for me. I shook the odd notion off and flicked the latch up, heaving the metal gates open. It was about time I tried it out for myself. In the evenings I'd jogged up the stairs to shake off the workday, but I didn't want to take on the stairs now.

The gates were heavier than I'd expected but once they got going the oiled wheels sped them on. Of course Armand was so much stronger than I, he made it look easy. As I locked the internal gate I realized I'd also missed the chance to ask his advice about my free time. Perhaps he'd gone away for the weekend. The thought made me realize just how much I'd enjoyed meeting him. It was such a good start to the day, being confined in *La Cage* with my sexy landlord.

As the elevator made its slow descent I felt

almost forlorn, not having seen him. Silly, really, but I couldn't help it. He was such a thrilling man to be around. Why was that? I wondered. His sexual magnetism, yes, but there was something else. As I stood in the metal cage, alone, it occurred to me that it was his air of utter self-control. He was a confident man, subtly commanding, too.

A shiver ran through me; a shiver of arousal. Would he be like that as a lover?

Yes, I just knew it. He'd be masterful.

I reached for a metal strut and held on, my senses running amok, my body stimulated by wild thoughts alone. I glanced at the staircase as the elevator passed through its spiral, imagining him walking down the steps, looking in at me as he did so. Even though he wasn't there, his presence haunted me.

When I retuned to the apartments that evening I noticed that Armand's Mercedes was parked opposite, and the window was wound down. As I got closer my breath caught, because I saw his reflection in the wing mirror. He climbed out of the car, tossing a pair of sunglasses onto the seat before closing the door.

As I glanced his way he smiled and waved,

then stepped across the road, joining me as I arrived at the steps up to the apartments. Had he been waiting, hoping to catch me? If it was a coincidence, it was uncanny.

"Good evening, fourth floor neighbor," he said.

"Good evening, fifth floor neighbor."

While we walked across the black-and-white checkered hall, side by side, it occurred to me that this was so much better than having seen him this morning, and I could ask him about the weekend after all.

"Shall we climb into *La Cage* together?"

Was it just his delicious French accent that made that sound so damned sexy, or did he mean it to sound like an overture to something entirely different than riding in the elevator with him? The suggestive undertow in his statements kept me on edge whenever we spent those precious few minutes together.

I nodded. "Although I'll have you know I managed it alone."

He paused before he closed the gates. "You in the cage, alone. How beautiful you must have looked, like an exotic bird." His eyes burned with his intensity. "I'm sorry I did not catch sight of you."

I could only stare at him, startled as I was by his comment. He really did think of this as a beautiful cage, and I was in it. The slow metal clanking sound as he hauled the gates together seemed to catch my very nerve endings, stringing them out with tension.

He took his time, controlling the complicated contraption, as ever. When the doors were secured he put his hand to the fifth floor button and pressed it. Then he rested back against the metal struts and folded his arms loosely across his chest. He looked at me, watchful as ever, if not more so.

He hadn't pressed the button for the fourth floor, my floor. Had he forgotten, or had he left me to do it on purpose, so that I'd have to reach over to his side of the space? He didn't seem the sort of person to forget, but maybe he had something else on his mind? My heart raced.

The cable mechanism whirred and after the longest moment, jolted into action. The elevator began its slow ascent. Still he didn't press the button. The only one lit up was for his floor. If he'd just forgotten, I'd look a twit when we shot past my floor.

The tension escalated.

"Oh," I said, as if I'd just remembered.

I reached over, but before I could press the button his hand covered it, stopping me.

"I thought you might like to come up to my apartment, share a bottle of wine and listen to some of the music you liked." He kept his hand over the button. The look in his eyes was so suggestive that there was no mistaking his intention. This wasn't just a casual neighborly invite.

So much for asking for his advice about what to do with my spare time. He'd derailed me, but onto a much faster track. My hand dropped to my side. I nodded. "I'd like that."

The way he had taken charge aroused me immensely.

We rode the rest of the way in silence. That prowling aura surrounded him again. Expectation built steadily inside me.

"Yours is the only apartment up here?" I said as we stepped onto the landing. There was only one door. It bore no number or name, unlike all the others in the block.

"Yes. The building belonged to my grandmother and when I inherited it I added this space, to make the most of the view, and the light."

As soon as he unlocked the door I saw what he meant. Despite the fact we were in a long hallway, a glass wall at the far end filled the space with amber light as the sun lowered over the city skyline.

"Come in, please."

I hadn't realized that I'd hesitated by the door, but I had. Nerves gathered in my belly. I'd stepped into his cage, and now I was going into his lair. I wanted to do it, but fear of the unknown had me in its grip.

When he led me into the lounge I found myself mesmerized by the massive space, and the view. Once again, tinted ceiling-to-floor glass gave way to a superb view across the rooftops of the city. Stepping through the room—which was furnished with black lacquered cabinets and low leather sofas—I put my laptop case and shoulder bag down and gazed out at the sight.

It was only when I heard the chink of glasses in the background I realized that he'd been busy. I heard wine sloshing into glasses, and then he switched on the stereo. Fusion music filtered up all around me, orchestral but with a samba beat. I turned back to him, ready to comment on the amazing view, but my words slipped away into nothing as I caught sight of the massive framed photographic print on the wall.

"Wow." My eyebrows lifted. Frozen to the

spot, I stared at the blatantly sexual image. It depicted a naked woman, starkly lit so that her body faded into darkness on one side. She was tethered by rope from above. The rope twined around her wrists, then back and forth across her torso, waist and hips. The way the rope was arranged seemed to emphasize her bared breasts and shaved pussy. She stared out of the image with fiery, accusing eyes. Thick, blunt-cut, bleached hair gave her a punky look

Armand watched on, as if waiting for me to say something. He'd removed his jacket. "Shibari, do you know it?"

I shook my head.

"It is the art of sensual rope work. Does it offend you?"

There was humor in his eyes.

He knew I wasn't offended. He knew exactly what I was. Horny, and getting hornier by the moment. It was as if he'd led me in here and stood me in front of this picture to get a reaction out of me, and he certainly had. Between my thighs I was hot and damp, my body bristling with uncertainty and expectation. I thought we were going to sip wine, chat and listen to the music, some kind of slow lead in. Instead I felt confronted—raw and edgy because I'd been thrust into a situation that both aroused and unnerved me.

When I didn't speak, he stepped closer to me. He put his finger under my chin and lifted my face, staring into my eyes as if examining my soul.

I swallowed, willing myself to act appropriately. "Is it your girlfriend?"

Was it an impertinent question? Maybe, but I didn't think so until it was out. I'd exposed my concern about territory and what was going on here.

"I like your directness, Jennie," he replied.

My directness was more blundering than intentional, but I wasn't about to tell him that.

"It's a friend," he continued. "We were lovers for a while, not anymore. She moved to the States. We shared the same interests, as you see." His gaze flickered to the image and back to me.

That was to the point. His interests included rope, and cages. I forced myself to look at the image again. Armand bound and displayed her that way. That much was obvious.

"It is art." His sensual mouth moved in a provocative smile.

It was art, yes. It was also blatantly kinky and erotic, but I wasn't going to be pedantic about it, not while he was touching me that way. Besides, the image thrilled and fascinated me.

Still he studied me, his fingers moving down the length of my throat. "Human nature intrigues me. We are greedy sometimes, we like to keep beautiful things as possessions, so that we can admire them, caged even."

He was so close I was sure he was about to kiss me.

"From the prettiest birds to rare, wild creatures…other people."

His knuckles moved around the curve of my breast, his touch all too vague and tantalizing through my clothing. "The urge to possess the thing we desire, even for a fleeting time, is great."

With his fingertips exploring me and his philosophical meandering about cages and possession, I was awash with desire. Over his shoulder, the blonde punk stared at me with those accusing eyes. I wanted to be displayed that way, naked and lewd and helpless—and so obviously his plaything. All the things he said to me about being caged, and the sound of the metal doors shunting together and apart as he handled them, filled my mind.

I thought he was going to kiss me, but although he looked at my lips, he didn't. Instead he asked

me another question, one that I wasn't expecting.

"Why did you come up here, Jennie?" His tone
was serious.

My heart raced erratically. "Because you
invited me."

He shook his head, and his eyes bored into
mine. "The real reason?"

Heat flared in my face. Unnerved by his serious tone I squirmed, my weight shifting from left
foot to right. I couldn't believe he was pushing
me to say it aloud. The attraction had been there
between us, but his sudden interrogation made
me feel awkward and obvious.

"You are so beautiful when you blush." His
expression softened. "The real reason you came
up here is because there is curiosity between us,
n'est-ce pas?"

"Yes, there is." It was hard to voice my
thoughts so blatantly and so soon, but the rush
I experienced having said it aloud was astonishing. It was liberating, and now that it was out
I felt as if we'd been shunted up to the next
level.

"Have you seen anything that surprised you?
The photograph, perhaps?" He'd reached inside
my jacket and was running the back of his

knuckles over the buttons on my shirt, as if he was readying to undo them.

"It did surprise me."

"It has that effect, but she was a willing submissive, believe me."

I bet she was. My eyelids flickered down, because I was unable to meet his bold stare a moment longer. I could scarcely believe it. He was touching me, questioning me provocatively while we stood there in his black lacquered bachelor pad, with its bleached bondage queen looking on, making me feel as if I couldn't ever be as good as her. A willing submissive. I could see why. The man made me melt just by looking at me. His touch would have me in a puddle of lust at his feet. But I also felt horribly inadequate and gauche.

"Perhaps I should go." I turned away, breaking the contact.

Armand put his hand on my shoulder, halting me. With the other he reached around and stroked my torso from collarbone to waist. The brusque, demanding nature of his touch stole my breath away. My eyes closed. When I moaned aloud, he eased me back to him. My upper body rested against the wall of his chest.

"Do you really want to go now, Jennie?" His

fingers moved inside the collar of my shirt, pushing it aside. His mouth was on my neck, then my collarbone, his kisses making me sizzle. "If you want to leave I'll let you go, but I don't think that's what you really want."

I could have stopped him then, he was making that obvious, but I didn't want to. His hips moved from side to side, slow and seductive, taking mine with them.

"No," I said, breathlessly. "I don't want to go, I'm just…" *Overwhelmed.*

It felt good, though, and I didn't want to be afraid to explore this. I wanted to know this masterful man who had shocked me several times over within the space of a few minutes.

With his hands locked on my shoulders, he turned me around and his mouth covered mine. Finally. His kiss melted me. My lips gave and his tongue moved between them. He devoured me, his tongue tasting my lips before thrusting into the damp cave of my mouth. I clutched at his shirt. My center ached, my clit throbbing wildly.

"I wanted you the moment I saw you," he whispered as he drew back. His voice was husky. He removed my jacket as he spoke, then his fingers went to my hair, easing it free of the clips that held it up. As it fell to my shoulders he murmured something in French.

I nodded. "It was the same for me."

My words seemed to act like a trigger on him, because he cursed in French. His eyes turned dark and his hands moved to my skirt. Without further ado he tugged it up, handling it roughly, until it was bunched at my waist. With his hands around my bottom he lifted me, wrapping my legs around his hips. I was so astonished that I clung to him, arms twined around his neck. One of my shoes fell to the floor. A moment later the other followed. The position he had put me in splayed my pussy against his hard erection. Unable to stifle my response, I gripped his shoulders and rocked my hips, rubbing against the hard, bulky protrusion.

His jaw clenched. He carried me easily, walking over to the long dining table that ran down the far side of the massive lounge. Resting me down on it, he eased my upper body flat to the table with his hand against my chest. "I think that first we must fuck, then we can play."

My body arched on the table. *Overwhelmed*.

I covered my eyes with the back of my wrist, moaning aloud at his blatant statement. He was going to have me on his dining table, right now.

"Unbutton your shirt." He stared at my stocking tops and his eyes flickered mischievously as if they were giving him ideas.

As I undid the buttons with trembling hands, he stripped off his own shirt and I had my first look at his body. I already knew from the way he'd lifted me so easily that he was strong, but his muscles were hard and defined, solid. He stared down at my groin and shook his head. "This must be done."

As soon as I got my shirt open, he bent to kiss me in the dip of my cleavage. My head rolled against the hard surface of the table. The way he took control made my pulse race and the damp heat between my thighs became sweltering. He tugged at the cups of my bra, pushing my breasts free of the fabric. He tongued one nipple, then the other, and the stiff points stung, making my hips squirm.

Armand lifted his head, put his hand between my thighs and cupped my pussy through my lace panties. Direct and demanding, it triggered a heightened need for release. The firm squeeze he gave me there at my pussy made me gasp aloud.

He trailed his fingers over my bare abdomen, which made me shiver. When I glanced down I saw a damp smudge on the front of the fabric. Pressing my lips together tightly, I moaned softly. Meanwhile Armand's eyebrows lowered, and his expression was brooding. When I glanced lower—and I couldn't help myself—I saw the bulge of his erection beneath the zipper on his jeans and my eyes flashed closed.

He ran his fingers beneath the band of my panties then tugged at them, pulling them down. I wriggled my bottom and lifted it to assist. When I was entirely naked, I squeezed my thighs together, suddenly aware that he had only removed his shirt. I felt so exposed.

"Open your legs," he instructed.

The way he said it made something hot coil and flex deep in my womb.

"Show me." He reached into his pocket, pulled out a condom packet and put it on the table.

I wanted to see him rip it open and roll it on. I wanted his hard cock ready to be inside me. It was the urgent sense of need that made me braver. I parted my thighs a couple of inches, exposing myself to him.

It was enough, Armand acted on it. First he inserted his fingers between my thighs and stroked them up and down over the soft, sensitive skin there. I began to pant, my hips rolling against the hard surface of the table. Still he stroked me. When the muscles in my thighs began to relax, he lifted my stockinged feet and put them flat to the table, forcing me to plant them wide apart, exposing my pussy fully. The sound of my blood rushing thundered in my ears. For several long moments that and the music were the only sounds in the room. Armand stood between my open legs in silence, apparently admiring me while I was so thoroughly debauched and displayed.

"Beautiful." He stroked his fingers up and down my damp folds.

I cried out, the tantalizing touch like torture when he made contact with my swollen clit. My hips rocked again. I wanted to rub myself against his hand, desperate for release.

"Easy." He arrested my jaw in one strong hand, making me meet his gaze. "I'm going to prepare you now," he whispered, "then I will fuck you, and I will need to do it hard."

The statement left me speechless, but I didn't need to respond because he ducked down and dipped his tongue into the damp groove of my pussy, rolling it back and forth over my swollen clit. The rush, the relief, the pleasure—for a moment I couldn't catch my breath. Then the lap of his tongue forced me to pant aloud. He had his hands planted either side of my hips on the table, his shoulders gleaming while his mouth engulfed my swollen clit—eating me from his dining table as if I was a delicious meal and he was a starving man.

His cologne and the scent of his body danced through my senses, making me want him even more. His hands were now wrapped around my buttocks as he lifted me to his mouth. The muscles in his shoulders rippled. All the while his words repeated in my mind, his promise to fuck me hard making me wilder still. My breasts ached, the nipples needling with sensation. My clit felt unbearably tight and hot, but his rapid tongue movements were pushing me ever closer. Then he grazed my tender flesh with his teeth and the release barreled through me. He pushed his tongue inside me, collecting my copious juices.

I was still gasping for breath when I heard him rip open the condom packet. I glanced down in time to see him rolling it the length of his erection, which arched up from his hips. My sex, still in spasm, clutched in anticipation. A moment later he hauled my hips closer to the edge of the table, moving me bodily across the surface so that I was positioned right at the edge and my legs dangled free. Never had I been so thoroughly manhandled, and never had I felt so deliriously high on something that I might consider base and primal if I was asked to think about it for too long.

When I felt the blunt head of his cock pushing at my slippery opening, my fingers curled into my palms. I remembered his warning. I wasn't ready. I felt too vulnerable—too exposed and sensitive, with my sex awash and swollen. But Armand had warned me, and he moved into position quickly, thrusting the hard length of his cock into me in one swift maneuver, stretching me, filling me and possessing me to the core.

"Armand!"

The pressure of his crown against my center sent an aftershock through my entire body. My torso lifted from the table, my hands latching on his shoulders.

He scarcely gave me a moment before he had me flat to the table again, my legs over his shoulders while he worked his length in and out of my sensitized sex, his hands on the table for purchase while he drove himself into me, relentlessly.

I was back at the precipice in moments, my groin alive with sensation.

The table was strong but shifted under us as he banged into me. His forehead gleamed, the depth and rhythm he maintained pushing us both closer. I could hear the slick pull of my wet pussy as he worked his cock in and out. My sex was sensitive to the point of being in pain, and yet it felt glorious. I was so close to coming again that my back arched and my fingernails bit into my palms.

Armand leaned closer still, bending my legs under him, his weight against my pussy. Again I flooded. The release was so great that I felt dizzy even though I was flat on my back, but the hard rod of his cock inside and the pressure of his body against my clit kept me there.

The muscles in his shoulders and neck stood out, his eyes closing.

His cock stiffened, stilled and jerked repeatedly. Another wave hit, my thighs shuddering as my every nerve ending was strung out with the raw pleasure of multiple orgasms brought on by this man.

He took me out to eat.

"You need sustenance," he said. "I will take good care of you, if you spend the weekend with me."

Sustenance for what? I wondered, remembering his comment about playing later. And now I was spending the weekend, not just the evening. Both fear and desire flared in my gut, making me tremble. I felt shell-shocked. He wasn't done with me yet. That certain knowledge was exhilarating. When we stepped out of the apartment block, the noise and lights of the city street seemed even more dazzling and exciting than they already were. I was high on the afterglow, and let him lead and guide me.

He took me to a small bistro two minutes walk away from the apartments. It was simple, and busy. As if aware of my heightened senses, he asked for a secluded booth at the back. There he sat alongside me, closing me into a world of our own. He ordered for us both and fed me delicacies with his fingers, while I sat looking at him in awe, accepting whatever he gave me. A couple of hours in his company, not much longer, and he'd mastered me so thoroughly.

The claret he ordered was good, and it made my muscles relax. Was that his intention? "The woman in the photograph…"

"Yes." He sat back and studied me as I spoke.

"She was a girlfriend?"

"Yes." He put his head on one side. "It bothers you?"

"No." It did. Of course it did. What woman

likes to see the gorgeous ex, even if this was only a one-night stand or a wild weekend or whatever it was. "I have no right, we're just…"

I looked away from our booth.

"Your hair is the color of honey," he said, drawing my attention back. He eased his finger through my thick mop, admiration shining in his eyes. When I met his gaze he shook his head. "You are what I want."

The simple statement did exactly what he meant it to.

It pushed away my doubts.

"I mean to enjoy you, thoroughly," he added. "If you are willing?"

The doubts had gone, but the nerves hadn't. Not completely.

Taking a deep breath, I nodded.

"Strip for me," he said when we went back to his apartment.

I glanced at the glass walls. "Can people see us?"

I'd been so caught up in the heat of the moment during our previous tryst that it hadn't even occurred to me. But now that we were back and he stood me deliberately at the center of the room, I felt very much on display. The lights were on and the city sky was dark above the rooftops.

"No. Only me."

My hands shook as I reached for the zipper on my skirt. I wanted to do it, but the concept of following a man's instructions regarding getting undressed was something I never thought I would ever do. It felt so good, though. At that moment I was under his command and loving it for as long as it lasted.

What did he intend to do with me? The question kept running back and forth through my mind, keeping me on edge and nervy. I took off my shirt. Kicking off my heels, I shuffled my skirt off then ran my thumb under the band on my lace undies, pausing.

He lifted one eyebrow.

"Will you…are you going to use the rope on me?"

"No." There was no hesitation in his voice. "Maybe another time," he added and smiled indulgently. Perhaps it had pleased him that I was curious about it. "I have something else in mind for you, something that will perhaps help you overcome your shyness about displaying yourself to me."

My attention was locked.

"Do you trust me to take care of you? That is very important."

Instinct led my judgment. "Yes, yes, I do."

"I am only interested in pleasure…extreme pleasure, yes, but I don't wish to hurt you. If I do, you must say so."

I swallowed my nerves. "I understand."

He studied me a moment longer. "It is your submission, your pleasure at my hands, that pleases me. I need to push your boundaries, in order to test my own."

My thumb was still caught in the band of my panties, and my fingers plucked at the fabric restlessly. "What do you have in mind?"

My voice was scarcely above a whisper.

"You will find out, when you strip for me." Humor lit his expression, warming me right through.

I reached around and undid my bra, peeling it off. When I cast it aside, he gestured again at my panties.

He wanted me there in that room again. Naked. Why in here? I was about to find out.

When I shoved my underwear down the length of my legs and stepped out of the abandoned lace, he nodded. I went for my lace stocking top and rolled the stocking down my leg. When I changed to the other leg he strolled behind me and stroked his fingers along the underside of my exposed buttock. The brief, provocative touch sent my nerve endings crazy. It was hard to keep undressing, but I had to.

Once entirely naked, I dropped the second stocking and presented myself.

Armand opened a drawer in one of his cabinets, and lifted out a slender stainless steel bar. Cuffs hung at either end of it. He held the slim metal bar out in front of me, his fist wrapped around it at the center point. "Offer me your wrists."

I did as instructed.

He did up the metal buckles that held the soft leather in place. I found my arms pushed apart by the object. I'd never seen anything like it and as I observed I realized I was now helpless. I couldn't move my hands unless he allowed me to.

When it was in place, he wrapped his fist around the middle between my hands, and lifted it, stretching my arms over my head. The movement was so sudden and so unexpected that I gasped aloud. My shoulders rolled and locked, my breasts lifting and then pushing together with the movement. Tension beaded down my spine.

He stared at me, then ran his free hand around my breasts.

My face heated. Unbearably self-conscious, I turned my head to one side.

"You flush so beautifully, because your skin is so pale."

I squirmed. No longer sure I could do this—even though I wanted to—I had to bite my tongue to stop from replying. Then his fingers locked on my uptilted nipple, and he fondled the stiff peak. Pain rang through me, delicious pain, like a heady intoxicant that made my groin heavy with longing. If I thought I'd been his plaything before, it had been nothing on this. He had complete control of me now. My head dropped back and I cried out.

His gaze drifted down my body and back up. "I intend to explore every part of you."

My skin was damp, everywhere, heat breaking out on the surface of my body. I lifted one foot, shifting my weight. I knew the look in my eyes was pleading, I meant it to be. "Please, Armand."

When I begged, he lowered his arm, tugged me right against him with the bar, and kissed me. Hard. Each time I felt the thrust of his tongue in my mouth my center ached for him to thrust there, too. The heat between my thighs had built, and I could feel the sticky tracts of my juices marking my inner thighs. My heart soared, the rush of raw emotion I felt for the way he handled me entwined with the real physical desire I felt. Breaking with the kiss, he led me with the bar, taking me to one corner of the room. There he lifted my arms above my head again, and latched the bar on to a hook that I had not previously noticed. I was at full stretch, my spine straight.

The room was his arena, his play den. The solid table, the cabinets and their contents, the hook. What else hadn't I noticed—what else was there to explore?

Armand stroked my body, taking full advantage of my helpless state to explore me. My skin was tingling wildly, everywhere, my nerve endings ragged. Then he lowered to a squat in front of me, ran his thumbs down my pussy, opening me up. Inside a heartbeat, his mouth had covered my clit. The metal restraint creaked when my body jerked. He stroked his tongue up and down over my clit. I was so sensitive from his earlier ministrations that I felt sure I would have pushed him away with my hands on his shoulders, had I been free. It was almost too much, and when his tongue rode back up, there was nothing I could do but submit.

"So sensitive! Armand…please…"

Back and forth his tongue went. It was as if he loved oral sex and couldn't get enough of me—either that or he wanted to drive me insane. My clit thrummed, and a wave of release hit me. I'd barely inhaled, and his fingers were thrusting into my sex. One of my legs lifted as I tried to pull away from the intense stimulation, my knee against the side of his head. When I glanced down I found him looking up at me with dark eyes, possessive eyes.

My legs shuddered. For a moment I hung limp in the restraint, allowing the hook to hold me up. I didn't care how I looked.

"Oh, yes, you're ready to offer yourself now."

Ready? Apparently he'd only just got started. How much more could I take? I'd never experienced such an intense barrage of stimulation, from pleasure to pain, desperation and embarrassment; it all hit me, tearing down my defenses and making me powerless and malleable in his hands.

He rose to his feet and held my waist. He kissed me and the pungent taste of my own arousal in his mouth made me aware of just how horny I was. How had this happened? I wondered vaguely as I let him possess me. Sex had never been like this before.

"The shame will soon be gone, all of it. Then you will only beg for the pleasure."

"Is that a threat or a promise?" I seriously wasn't sure. My current state was a combination of bliss, acute arousal and humiliation, the latter because his mouth was so heavy with my musk.

He gave a husky laugh. "A promise." He ran his thumb over my cheek. "Freedom from shame is a wonderful gift, you will know this soon."

Leaving me with that thought, he strolled off to his cabinet. When he came back he had a second slim bar in his hands.

What the hell was he going to do with that?

He unhooked me, lowering my arms. My shoulder ached, but it felt good, like a long workout or a sports massage.

Armand gestured at the floor. "On your hands and knees."

Swallowing my nerves, I lowered to my knees. The carpet was thick under my bare knees. I put my hands out to balance myself, moving awkwardly within the restraint.

I saw his shirt drop to the floor. Then he squatted in front of me, and lifted my chin with one finger. With a swift move he brought a glass to my lips. I looked into his eyes as I sipped gratefully at the cold water he offered.

"Enough?"

I nodded. He took the glass away. When he returned he'd shed the rest of his clothing. My breath caught in my throat as I looked up at his magnificent body.

A moment later he stepped behind me and his hands enclosed my ankles, hauling them apart. I felt him move the cold metal under my feet. He moved my legs further apart before he tied my ankles in place.

I muttered incoherently when I realized how exposed my rear end was, every part of it on display to him. Squirming—with my head hanging down and my hair obscuring my face—my body reacted, my sex tightening. When it did, moisture ran down between my folds, which only made my situation worse. I tried to move forward to gain my equilibrium, but the friction of the carpet on my knees made me realize just how useless my attempts were. I swayed, my breasts dangling lewdly.

"Please," I begged, desperate for him to take control of me and bring me release.

He walked around me, surveying the scene. At

first I cared about how I must look, but then his gaze on me while I was so vulnerable and help-less made me burn up with longing, and I didn't care anymore. I thrust my pussy out between my open legs, lifting my hips in the air, needful and restless and apparently now shameless.

Armand whispered words of approval in French. I could scarcely breathe. When he circuited me again his cock was at full stretch, its crown gleaming. He seemed able to ignore it, while he took his time studying my body. Wasn't that what I had wished for, though, to be lewdly displayed just like the bondage queen in the photo? Well, she'd got off lightly. He'd pushed me in a different direction altogether. Confront-ing my shyness about my body he'd put me in this position, arms and legs apart, every part of me exposed and vulnerable.

He paused in front of me and when I looked up at him, curious, he rode his fist up and down his hard cock. His jaw was tight, his eyes narrowed. The tight muscles of his abs were standing out, his belly a hard rock of tension.

My mouth watered for a taste of him. "May I…may I taste you?"

His eyes glittered, his eyebrows drawn down as he concentrated. His only response was to direct his cock head to me. Rising up on my knees, I first rested my cheek against the hot surface of his shaft, moving my face against him adoringly. Then I licked him, eagerly absorbing the fecund taste of his cock. When I ran my tongue up and down the shaft, he growled in his throat. Taking the swollen head into my mouth, I closed my eyes and sucked, my tongue lapping around the head before I shifted and took as much length into my mouth as I could.

"Enough." He pulled free.

I felt his hand on my back, directing me to my former position, on hands and knees. I wavered, panting for breath, but lit up with the knowledge that he was going to mount me now. At my back, I heard him rip open a condom packet. All of it impacted on my senses, making me restless as an animal in my restraints, my body undulating, pussy pushed back and out expectantly.

"You want this?" He let me feel the weight of his cock against my hot niche.

"Please," I begged. "Desperate for you." I hung my head.

He entered me, giving me a couple of inches, then held back.

Tears smarted in my eyes.

"What do you need?"

"You," I whimpered, moving my hands uselessly within the restraints.

He gave me another inch. "What do you really want…what is your most basic need at this moment?"

"But…"

"Say it, admit it."

"I need to come," I blurted. "But only because you put me in this state!" I shot that over my shoulder. I had to say it, to blame him, because it was true.

Armand laughed softly. He stroked me at the base of my spine, soothing me. I felt affection in his touch. Then he held my hips, and— mercifully—gave me his full length.

He drove into me with more caution than before, seemingly aware of how sensitive I would be, but once his cock was bedded deep within me his hands roved over my buttocks and he pulled them apart, his thumbs stroking over my exposed seam.

It drove me wild.

Earlier on I'd reflected that I'd never been handled this way. Now I realized I'd never been treated this way, forced to address my animal need for pleasure—and Armand was right. It did feel good, desperately good.

Armand was gentler with me. This time it was me who couldn't hold back—it was me who worked him. He stroked my body, caressing my spine while I took what I needed, driving back on to his hard shaft. He reached around and fondled my dangling breasts, then tugged on my nipples.

All the while I chased the prize, riding the long slick erection that he offered, working myself with the restraints to use it well. I wriggled and squirmed, my hips moving back and forth against him, mewling loudly as my sensitive flesh milked him off in rhythmic clutches.

"Oh, yes, Jennie, it's good, very good," he said, his cock jerking.

I'd made him come, and I'd reached the point of sheer ecstasy. My sex clenched over and over. My body was free from decorum, unleashed, until finally it was a blur of sensation and nothing more.

I didn't leave Armand's apartment again that weekend. He told me I didn't need to because the weekend was "ours." He had food delivered, and he cooked for me. It was as if he was happy to keep me as his private plaything, and I was thrilled to be that. Paris could wait until another weekend.

He went to my apartment to collect my toiletries, refusing to let me fetch them myself. While he left me alone, he handcuffed me to the wrought-iron headboard of his bed. It should have felt wrong, but it didn't. The way he cherished me overruled any possibility of that. When he returned he claimed me back by kissing me, everywhere.

The weekend passed in a glorious haze of sensory overload.

On Monday morning, at seven, reality forced its way back in. I had forty-five minutes until I had to be on my way to the embassy. With regret I kissed him and climbed out of his bed, running around in my shirt and panties, barefoot, trying to find my belongings. I needed to get back to my own apartment and prepare for the working day ahead.

When I darted into the lounge, however, I was once again frozen to the spot.

My shoulder bag dropped from my hand as I stared at the blank place on the wall where the image of the blonde bondage queen had been. It was no longer there. I glanced around, but couldn't see it standing anywhere. Armand must have taken it down when I was asleep.

My heart fluttered. Why had he done that?

He followed me in a moment later, still heavy with sleep. He wore his nakedness with complete nonchalance, prowling over to me. He arrested me in a lazy but possessive embrace, covering my face with hungry kisses.

His large hands on my bottom pressed my hips to his, and I felt the bough of his erection against my belly.

"Armand, please. I must go and prepare for work."

"You will come back to me tonight?"

"If you want me to." I couldn't keep the smile from my face.

He returned it then nodded his head back in the direction of the space on the wall where the photograph had been. "I need your help to select some new art."

He had taken it down for me. It was a significant gesture.

I laced my fingers around his neck, brimming with happiness, suddenly willing to let another few moments slide away in order to give this the attention it deserved.

"I'd love to," I responded, and then lifted my eyebrows, "or perhaps we could make some art of our own…?"

Armand growled as he ducked to kiss my jaw.

Over his shoulder, I looked at the blank space on the wall and my mind ran wild with ideas. My six months in Paris promised to be a voyage of discovery, and with Armand as my master, I was ready and willing for every moment of it.

12 Shades left you wanting more?

Read on for an exclusive extract of Megan Hart's emotional, unforgettably erotic full-length story – *Switch* – available *now*!

Switch

By Megan Hart

Shall we begin?

This is your first list.

You will follow each instruction perfectly. There is no margin for error. The penalty for failure is dismissal.

Your reward will be my attention and command. You will write a list of ten. Five flaws. Five strengths.

Deliver them promptly to the address below.

The square envelope in my hand bore the faint ridges of really expensive paper and no glue on the flap, like the reply envelope included with an invitation. I turned the heavy, cream-colored card that had been inside it over and over in my fingers. It felt like high-grade linen. Also expensive. I fingered the slightly rough edge along one side. Custom cut, maybe, from a larger sheet. Not quite heavy enough to be a note card, but too thick to use in a computer printer. I lifted the envelope to my face and sniffed it. A faint, musky perfume clung to the paper, which was smooth but also porous. I couldn't identify the scent, but it mingled with the aroma of expensive ink and new paper until my head wanted to spin.

I touched the black, looping letters. I didn't recognize the handwriting, and the letter bore no signature. Each word had been formed carefully, each letter precisely drawn, without the careless loops, ticks and whorls that marked most people's writing. This looked practiced and efficient. Faceless. The paper listed a post-office box at one of the local branch offices, and that was it. Since moving into Riverview Manor five months ago, I'd received a few advertising circulars, requests for charitable donations addressed to two different former tenants and way too many bills. I hadn't had any personal mail at all. I turned the card over again, listening to the soft sigh of the paper on my skin. It didn't have a name or address on the front. Only a number, scrawled in the same languid hand as the note. I looked closer, seeing what in my haste I hadn't noticed before.

***

That explained it, then. This note wasn't for me at all. The ink had smeared a little, turning the one into a passable version of a four, if you weren't paying close attention. Someone had stuffed this into my mailbox, *414,* by mistake. At least it wasn't another baby shower or wedding invitation from "friends" I hadn't seen in the past few years. I wasn't a fan of being put on a loot-gathering mailing list just because once upon a time we'd been in a math class together.

"What's that?" Kira had come up behind me in a cloud of cigarette odor and now dug her chin into my shoulder. I don't know why I didn't want to show her, but I closed the card and slipped it back into the envelope, then found the right mailbox and shoved it through the slot. I peeked into the glass window and saw it resting inside the metal cave, slim and single and alone.

"Nothing. It wasn't for me."

"C'mon then, whore. Let's get upstairs. We have a threesome with Jose, Jack and Jim." She held up the clanking paper grocery sack containing the bottles. Every woman should have a slutty friend. The one who makes her feel better about herself. Because no matter how drunk she got the night before, or how many guys she made out with at that party, or how short her skirt is, that slutty friend will always have been…well…sluttier. Kira and I had traded that role back and forth over the years, a fact I would never be proud of but couldn't hide.

"It's not even eight o'clock. Things don't start jumping until at least eleven."

"Which is why I stopped at the liquor store." She looked around the lobby and raised both eyebrows. "Wow. Nice." I looked, too. I always did, even though I'd memorized nearly every tile in the floor.

"Thanks. C'mon, let's grab the elevator." She had to have been as equally impressed with my apartment, but she didn't say so. She swept through it, opening cupboard doors and looking in my medicine cabinet, and when it came time to eat the subs we'd bought for dinner she made a show of setting my scarred kitchen table with real plates instead of paper. But she didn't tell me it was nice.

It was almost like old times as we giggled over our food and watched reality TV at the same time. I hadn't forgotten what a bizarre and hilarious sense of humor Kira had, but it had been a long time since I laughed so hard my stomach clenched into knots. I was suddenly glad I'd invited her over. There's something nice about being with someone who already knows all your faults and likes you anyway…or at least doesn't like you any less because of them.

She had a new boyfriend. Tony something-or-other, I didn't recognize the name. Kira had never mentioned him in her text messages or occasional e-mails to me, but the way she dropped it casually into our conversation now meant she wanted me to ask about him.

"How long have you been going out?" I leveled a shot of Cuervo and studied it, not sure I wanted to take it. Once upon a time I'd been able to toss them back without fear of the consequences, but I hadn't done much drinking lately. I pushed it toward her, instead.

Kira drank back the shot with a practiced gulp. "Since just after you moved. A long time."

I didn't feel as if it had been that long, but anything longer than three months was a record of sorts with her. "Good for you."

She wrinkled her nose. "Whatever. He's good in bed and buys me shit. And he has a fucking awesome car. He's got a job. He's not a loser."

"All good things." I had slightly higher standards, or at least now I did, but I smiled at her description of him and wrapped up the papers from our food.

Kira got up to help me. "Yeah. I guess so. He's a good guy." Which said more than anything else she had. I shot her a look. Times did change, I reminded myself. So did people. When it came time to get ready to go out, though, the Kira I knew faked a gag. "Gawd, don't wear that."

I looked down at my low-rise jeans. They were boot cut. I had boots. I even had a cute cap-sleeved T-shirt. The hours of working out I'd been putting in lately were paying off. "What's wrong with what I have on?"

Kira swung open my closet door and rummaged around inside. "Don't you have anything…better?"

High school was a long time ago, I wanted to say, but looking at her short denim skirt and tight, belly-baring blouse, I figured my comment would be lost. I shrugged, instead. "I know you have hotter clothes than that." Kira reappeared from my closet with a handful of shirts and skirts I remembered buying but hadn't worn in a long time. She tossed the clothes onto my bed, where they spread out in a month's worth of outfits.

I picked up a silky tank top in a pretty shade of lavender and a stretchy black skirt. I held them up to myself in front of my full-length mirror. Then I put them back on the bed. "No, thanks,"

I said. "I'll wear what I've got on. It's comfortable." Kira shook her head. "Oh, ew. Paige, c'mon."

"Ew?" I looked at myself again. The jeans clung to my hips and ass just right, and my T-shirt emphasized how flat my stomach was becoming. I thought I looked pretty damn good. "What's ew?"

"It's just, you know…" Kira trailed off and pushed her way next to me to hog the reflection. "You gotta show off a little bit."

I looked her over. Even in my stack-heeled boots, I stood a few inches shorter. She'd grown her natural red hair into long layers that fell halfway down her back. She never tanned, so her dark eyeliner looked extra black and the fuck-me red lipstick even redder.

I looked in the mirror again, turning my chin to one side, then the other, to catch my profile. My hair's blond. And it's natural. My eyes are blue, but dark, almost navy. I look a lot like my dad, which is one reason, maybe, why he never bothered denying I was his.

"I think I look fine," I told her, but the faint sound of longing slithered into my voice.

I spent my clothes budget on simple, brand-name pieces I picked up off-season or in discount stores. I'd spent the past few years building my wardrobe. Clothes for work and casual wear that looked expensive enough to pass as classy. I paired them with shoes I couldn't always afford. I wasn't going to be Clarice Starling, giving away my background with my good bag and my cheap shoes.

I looked again at my reflection and thought of the whisper of satin on my skin. Going without a bra, how my nipples would push at the fabric and force a man's eyes straight to my breasts. Every man's eyes.

I picked up the tank top again and held it up. I smoothed the fabric over my stomach. Kira gave me an approving nod and slung an arm around my shoulders and bumped me with her hip. "C'mon. You know you want to."

I did want to. I wanted to go out and get shit-hammered drunk and dance and smoke and rub up on half a dozen boys. I wanted to feel a hot, hard body against mine and look for lust in a pair of eyes I didn't know.

I wanted not to worry about proving anyone right about me.

I pulled my tank top over my head and after a second's hesitation, unhooked my bra. The satin tank top slithered over my head and fell to my hips. My breasts swayed under the smooth fabric. My nipples tightened at once, and I shivered.

"Let me get you some makeup," Kira said.

She lugged her huge purse over to me and pulled out pots and tubes and brushes and glitter. I love glitter. I hadn't worn glitter in forever, either. No place for it here, in my new life. "I'll do it." I wouldn't dream of sharing makeup that had been on her face. No telling what germs could be passed on that way. I waved her away and went into my bathroom, where I rummaged beneath my sink.

I pulled out my own box of tricks and treats. Lipsticks in berry shades, eye shadows in rainbow hues. Lots and lots of half-used black-eyeliner sticks and a few bottles of liquid eyeliner. I shook one, thinking it must have dried up after all these years, but when I unscrewed the cap with its built-in brush, the makeup inside was still smooth.

I painted a mask. It looked just like me, only brighter. Bolder. More. Once, I'd worn this face every day. Once, it had been the only one I had.

My makeup finished, I squeezed into the tight black skirt. I left my legs bare. I'd be chilly on the walk from the parking garage to the bar, but hot enough inside once I started dancing. From my closet I pulled out a truly fucking fabulous pair of pumps. Kira had been bent over her phone, fingers stabbing out messages, but her eyes widened and she reached for the shoes. "Oh, wow. Steve Madden!"

"First pair I ever bought." I stroked the smooth black patent leather. Four-inch heels. Most men couldn't have told the difference between a Steve Madden shoe and a Payless pump, but they looked twice when I wore them. Sometimes more than twice.

I slipped into the shoes and stood, adjusting to the way my center of balance shifted. My mother had taught me the art of how to walk in heels this high. I used to raid her closet as a kid and parade around the house in her shoes. I smoothed the silky shirt over my belly and hips and turned around to look at myself one last time in the mirror.

"Ready to go?"

"I guess so," Kira said sullenly. "Except now you look awesome and I look like shit."

"You look hot," I promised. What were friends for? She was convinced, more because she wanted to believe it than because I'd tried hard. "Okay, let's go get shit-hammered!"

***

I saw him again, that dark-haired man. This time, he was coming in as I was going out. We passed each other not so much like two ships, as much as one ship passing while the other crashes into an iceberg. I couldn't be offended that his gaze slid over and past me, taking in the short skirt and high heels without a second look. He had his head down and was talking urgently into his cell phone. He didn't have attention to spare me. And it wasn't his fault I was trying so hard to pretend I wasn't looking back at him that I ran into the edge of the door frame hard enough to leave a bruise.

"Smooth move, Ex-Lax." Kira smirked. She hadn't even noticed it was the man from earlier that day. "Nice to see you can hold your tequila."

I shrugged off the sting in my shoulder and didn't reply. His sleeve had brushed my bare arm as he passed, and the hairs on it all the way up to the back of my neck had stood at that brief, simple touch. A slow, tumbling roll of sensation centered in my belly. He lived in my building.